DEBRIS SEA
AND OTHER SCIENCE FICTION STORIES

Nicholas Licalsi

STEP INTO THE ROAD

For my friend John Middleton.

I still reverberate with excitement and encouragement from that first high five you gave me when I told you I was a writer.

Thank You Patrons!

There's nothing quite like the magic of exploring new worlds and
meeting unique characters through storytelling.
And there's *absolutely* nothing like the magic of knowing that there
are people willing to support that expedition.
These stories are my bounty. I know you'll enjoy them.

Katelyn Combs, Bonnie, BW, Melinda Callender,
Roy & Beth Shockey, Sam Meeks, John Middleton, Matt VanNatten.

Join the team at: https://patreon.com/stepintotheroad

Contents

Miscalculations

Miscalculations will get you every time. Even with the smartest AIs, custom-designed equipment, and the most complex bureaucracies, something always gets overlooked. But the engineer who designed this custom dome wasn't the one drenched in sweat due to their oversight.

Instead, I was. I lay on our thin foam mattress, sheets crumpled at our feet, with my tank top tucked between my stomach and my breasts to keep my skin from uncomfortably sticking to itself. My long hair was tied up in a high ponytail because I was sick of it clinging to the back of my neck. I was wide awake late in the night considering if I should cut it pixie short like Chanda had.

Beautiful Chanda who was lying next to me, miraculously asleep. Or at least acted like she was sleeping. I knew for sure at least one person in this tiny room wasn't acting: Artie.

If she was awake and uncomfortably hot, we would know about it. The neighbors would know about it. The whole dome would know about it. That baby had lungs and wasn't afraid to use them.

We lovingly called our room a cell because it was a perfect four-meter cube with smooth LED walls that popped out when you needed to access the few storage cupboards or perform maintenance on the utility equipment.

The walls gave off a soft blue glow as they displayed a simulated starry sky at night, anything to make us feel like we had more space than we did. During the day the walls were decorated with shifting images of our family, or an endless Arcadian forest, or cheesy space station noir films that Chanda and I had fallen in love over in college. Soon they'd show bright-colored animated animals teaching letters and numbers. Equally cheesy, but I'd enjoy them just as much for the other girl I loved.

Artie was lying in the auto-rocking crib, its bars yet another thing simulating a prison around her. We'd checked out the crib from the storeroom when she was born, along with countless other pieces of baby paraphernalia. We'd keep it for the next year and a half until she was big enough to get a toddler bed and the three of us moved into a two-bedroom cell. The toys and crib that once belonged to Artie would be passed to the next family that had a baby.

I tried not to look forward to the extra space. I tried not to wish Artie's life away in the pursuit of receiving more space in this cramped dome. But it was hard when there was only so much to go around on this desert planet.

The room still smelled like curry from dinner, and the many dinners before tonight. Chanda had picked up her favorite yellow curry from the commissary, and because of that, I could still feel the spice tingling on my tongue. We ate it as a family around the table that rose up out of the titanium floor. The same floor that produced this shallow bed when we were ready to sleep.

If it wasn't for Artie's toys, playpen, and highchair this room would be empty. Everything stored away into one hidden compartment or another. The baby brought life into the cell in more ways than one.

"I can't keep living like this," I whispered into the night.

"Neither can I," Chanda replied. "But one day we'll be free, Letty. More land than any of our ancestors could have imagined."

We were not being held against our will. We were not being punished, despite the torturous heat. Chanda and I had agreed to join this terraforming project. There were promises of payment in the form of green land and the challenge of using our degrees. The only person who hadn't agreed to be here was Artie. But we hoped that the future we were bringing her into was far more promising than a future on the crowded Feldman's station where Chanda and I grew up.

Tonight's uncomfortable heat had been politely explained in a memo last week. Due to the added humidity from the terraforming project, the moisture held more heat into its new atmosphere. All promising and necessary for a hospitable world. However, a miscalculation–oversight from the engineering team that designed our dome didn't take this trapped heat into account. Meaning the cooling utilities didn't work as efficiently as expected.

The memo briefly noted, as if it was of no real concern to anyone, that rooms sharing a wall with the dome's exterior heat shield would be a tad hotter. Only a few families shared a wall with the shield. Unfortunately, our family was one of them.

The memo concluded with reassurances that no one would suffer from heatstroke and that our ancestors would get to enjoy the most idyllic summers imaginable once our efforts were complete. I just wished I could be dreaming of those summers, instead of being wide awake.

"I talked to Quartermaster Erikson today," I whispered. "He said we're on the list for an extra coolant pump but currently they're all checked out."

Over the past ten-day week, I'd become all but an expert on cooling utilities and coolant pumps and everything else that controlled the atmosphere in our sealed dome. The quick and easy fix was to lend us a coolant pump, it was the size of a human leg and blew cold air out of the top like an old city fountain.

Unfortunately, those had been checked out earlier, before the memo. Young couples like us ignored the heat, thinking it was a passing fad. Old couples who were quick to complain loudly when their environment budged half a degree snapped up all the coolant pumps from the quartermaster. Maybe their old age made them persnickety, more likely it made them wise enough to know to complain early so they weren't last in line like us.

"It's not like we can climb the wait list faster," Chanda said. "Keep talking to Erikson. Stay top of mind. He'll eventually get us one."

"I could do that. Or we could steal some coolant."

Chanda let out a laugh followed by a snort followed by a quiet gasp. We both looked hesitantly towards to auto-rocker.

When Artie didn't make a peep and the coast was clear we rekindled our conversation.

"Think about it," I said. "We're uniquely suited to steal something from the storeroom."

"We'd get in trouble. We'd be going over the quartermaster's head."

"They're not going to kill us, or ship us back to the station over it."

"No, they'll dock our land grant, maybe void it entirely. We'd be the only people on the planet that aren't landowners. Plus, we'd be taking away a coolant pump from some other family."

Being an engineer with access to manuals for every single object on in the dome had its advantages. As dull as some of those manuals were I was highly motivated to find a solution to this heat problem.

In my research, I found that there were other ways to cool down a room. Ancient ones like ceiling fans which would be impossible to install in the smooth LED ceiling of the cell and would only move the musty hot air around. But there was also a way to supercharge the cooling utility that was hidden behind one of the wall compartments between the fold-out desk and Chanda's slide-out wardrobe.

"Look, you're a chemist, you've got access to the sector of the storeroom where they store the fluorocarbon. Fluorocarbon we can use to supercharge the cooling utility. I've got access to the engineering equipment to store it as we transport it from your lab to the cell. Then we're ice cubes by this time tomorrow night."

"No. No. No. I'm not putting us and our daughter's future at risk because you're too hot to sleep comfortably."

"I didn't leave Feldman's to have a life that's even worse than the one we would've had there," I said in that strained raspy voice one uses when trying to shout and whisper at the same time. "It's a victimless crime. The fluorocarbon will get released and captured by the air circulator and be stored back in your lab. No one will know it's gone."

"Someone will know it's gone Letty," she said. "The quartermasters always know when things go missing in the dome."

I rubbed Chanda's leg affectionately with mine and even if she was a bit warm, I didn't mind. "You remember when we snuck into the Astroboi concert junior year? They were playing in the station's botanical gardens and the tickets were too expensive for us."

"You said the same thing then: it's a victimless crime. Claimed they were playing whether or not we were there, we weren't stealing anything."

"And it went down smoothly."

"Because I was there to flirt with the gardener who saw us sneak in through his utility entrance."

"Exactly, that young man was lucky to get the time of day from you. If anything, I was the victim because of how that interaction between you two strained my heart."

"And supercharging the cooling utility is safe?" Chanda asked, ignoring my jest.

"It's no more complicated than my monthly visits to replace terra-gas containers at the outposts."

"And you're sure we can't ask the quartermaster to just do this for us?" Chanda asked. "He checks out some fluorocarbon and we go about this through the right channels."

"If Erikson did it for us then he'd have to do it for everyone. There wouldn't be enough fluorocarbon to go around. But there weren't enough coolant pumps to go around either so what we're doing isn't different from what's already been done."

"Fine," Chanda agreed. "But only because without me you'll get yourself into trouble."

I let out a small, childish, squeal of glee and rolled to her side of the bed to kiss her. Chanda's lips were soft and warm like a cup of chai tea.

Unfortunately, Artie was not as deep asleep as I'd thought and she started whining. I peeled myself off Chanda and rolled off my side of the bed to comfort the little girl. We didn't need her bringing any unnecessary attention to ourselves tonight.

***

There were only so many resources on the planet and most of them were inside the large dome that every human on the planet lived in. Sure, we took shuttles to the outposts where tall wiry towers released terraforming gas into the atmosphere in an effort to eventually make it hospitable but each of those trips, even the ones on the other side of the world, took a day, maybe 26 hours round trip.

And all of those limited supplies were kept in the fractal hallways of this storeroom. A main hallway split into four orthogonal hallways like a capital H. Then each of those four hallways had even more shorter hallways splintered off of those. These splintered hallways were a quarter the size of our cell but instead of storing furniture in the floor and being littered with baby toys, these walls had compartments that slid out like drawers and shelves that rose out of the ground.

If you requested something a little red line would appear on the wall and like a fairy it would lead you through the rooms. That's assuming that you hadn't temporarily disabled the AI and were taking something that you didn't want logged.

Since I'd disabled the AI, the entire room was giving off a faint blue light as the screensaver for the walls, a navy blue with sine waves of light blue running down the halls in a seemingly random pattern. Luckily there was nothing popped out of the ground, otherwise, I'd be tripping on everything.

There weren't any security cameras in the storeroom for the same reason there weren't any security cameras in the commissary or the cells or the bathrooms. There were about a half dozen humanitarian treaties that set very strict limits on when citizens, employees, and people could be monitored. And a city-sized dome was not on that list of approved locations. People needed space to conduct their lives and trust wasn't that hard to give, especially when everything was provided for through the quartermasters.

Everything except cool living quarters.

Some people thought the treaties were put in place by thugs looking to get away with crimes all over the galaxy. Some thought that it was overly liberal humanitarian groups lobbying with an idealized trust of their fellow citizens. Right now, I didn't care, I was just glad it was one less thing to solve in this little heist.

Chanda dipped into a cubby off the main hallway we were walking down. I thudded along in my heavy work boots to catch her.

I was in a dark blue jumpsuit that I used for work repairing various equipment, bots, and vehicles that were used for terraforming the planet. My boots thumped on the hollow spots in the ground, where shelves would rise up. There were supposed to be little aisles where one could walk without making much noise. The quartermaster knew where they were but I never did.

Chanda's shoes were quieter little flats that were thin and quiet. She still had on the lab coat over a pair of silky pants and a frilly blouse. She kept the lab coat on just because she was working with chemicals. She was a stickler for the rules, all things considered. And following behind her I could smell the citrus perfume that she wore and it led me through the hallways to the chemist sector of the storeroom.

I was nervous. I could still taste the extra cup of coffee I'd had before ending my shift early. I thought it'd keep me awake and alert for this little heist. I hadn't gotten much sleep the night before, partially the heat, partially running through this plan again.

I had a four-liter metal tank under my arm. It had been emptied some time ago. The engineers kept a pile of cleaned empties in a corner of the dock garages.

The tanks probably should've gone back to the storeroom. But then we'd be making trips from the exterior docks to the interior storeroom and that was a waste of time. And that laziness was lucky for me.

The tank wasn't much bigger than Artie. Although it was significantly lighter than her. Luckily for this little project, it wasn't apt to cry or coo at me if something went awry.

I joined Chanda in the small hallway. It felt cramped with the walls showing their dark screensaver. Normally they'd be bright white with lots of helpful labels and images. The whiteness made rooms feel bigger, even when you still knew you could stand in the middle and touch each wall with your fingertips.

Chanda pressed on the wall. With a pneumatic hiss, a long row of brass nozzles extended into the middle of the room.

She looked over them carefully and eventually pointed at one. "This is what you need."

"How'd you know?" To me, they all looked identical. Plus, there were probably a dozen rows of nozzles stored in the walls, all plumbed to various gasses.

"They're manually labeled," she said pointing to some chemist markings I didn't understand. "And I looked up which row we needed this morning."

"Couldn't do it without you," I said giving her a quick peck on the cheek and then hooking the empty tank up to the nozzle.

"No, you couldn't," she said. She walked to the entrance of the room looking down the long hallway that led to this one.

The fluorocarbon was scentless, or at least the seal was firm enough that nothing escaped into the air. But the long row of nozzles did have a faint oily lubricant smell. Probably to keep it running in and out smoothly.

The tank grew heavy as it filled up with the fluorocarbon. It wasn't too much to carry but it was starting to outweigh even Artie. I didn't look forward to the little girl being too big for me to carry safely in my arms.

The entire room lit up bright white and for a moment I thought I'd gone blind, or something had blown up in my face.

Unfortunately, someone had just entered the room without disabling the AI. A bright red line ran down the hallway connecting whoever was walking through here with wherever they needed to go.

I cursed and unscrewed the tank and sent the nozzles back into the wall. Chanda looked at me worried. We could hear the deep voice of Quartermaster Erikson carrying through the hallways. He was going on about the various options that were available for whatever equipment the person he was helping needed. It was a familiar conversation. We'd had it recently.

The red line passed right outside the room we were in. There was no door to seal shut and hide behind. The voices were still in the main hallway, we had to get past the end of the red navigation line if we had any chance to hide.

"Run," I said tucking the tank in my arms like I was rushing down the hall holding Artie herself.

My boots echoed on the hollow parts of the floor, parts that I should've avoided. But Erikson was a loud and boisterous talker, he was precise about his inventory but not much else. Chanda was running next to me, I followed the red line down the hall, it seemed to go on forever.

Suddenly Erikson's voice became very loud. It wasn't shouting at us to stop...yet. I ducked into a cubby and yanked Chanda with me. I almost dropped the tank since it was nearly too heavy to carry under one arm.

I looked around the room, it was familiar enough. Pictures of auto-rockers, strollers, and high chairs were displayed on the bright white walls.

Along with a bright red line that ran straight into the room and pointed to a drawer labeled with images of diaper cleaner, since diapers were reusable there was of course a special machine to clean them.

"You pulled us into the room they're headed towards," Chanda said in a raspy angry whisper.

"We were out of time. Grab some blankets," I said.

Chanda gave me a brief look of confusion before I looked away searching for something that might help us out of this mess. My eyes landed on the image of a plastic black stroller. Its wheels were painted silver like a rover's. Its cradle-like seat would fit Artie perfectly. The crib also had an unnecessary umbrella over it. Well unnecessary inside the dome but hopefully very necessary once the planet was terraformed.

I pressed on the stroller compartment and it popped out with another pneumatic hiss and the smell of lubricant. Five strollers were filed away and folded up neatly.

I set the tank on the metal ground.

The tank meeting the metal let out a thud.

Erikson's voice was close and it paused for a moment as if he was trying to figure out if he'd imagined the sound.

I wrapped my hands around the metal to silence the ringing as best I could.

Once it quieted down and Erikson's deep voice started again and I pulled out a stroller. I had to quickly unfold it from its compact storage state. I could repair a rover's nuclear engine, disassemble a terra-gas disperser, and operate hydraulic equipment big enough to lift ten times my weight. But this plastic baby equipment got me every time.

Chanda, my lovely savior, shoved the blankets into my arms and finished unfolding the stroller. I wrapped the tank up in the blankets faster than I would ever dare wrap up Artie.

Erikson entered the room his voice louder than ever going on and on about why the reusable diapers couldn't go in the community disposal system. A lecture we'd heard at least three times by now.

I turned my back to the opening holding the tank close against my chest like it was a baby.

"Oh, I didn't realize there was anyone else in the storeroom," Quartermaster Erikson said.

"We didn't want to bother you, we just needed a stroller for Artie," Chanda said pushing the stroller behind her and in front of me. "We were going to take her through the gardens but she's getting so big so quick and it's hard to carry her for long walks now."

"I understand," Erikson said.

I placed the tank in the little stroller and the cradle sagged under the weight of the tank. It wasn't noticeable unless you were really looking for it. But to be safe I pulled the little umbrella forward to hide the fake baby. I hoped Erikson wouldn't notice the unnecessary decision.

I stepped behind the stroller and smiled at Erikson who was standing next to a pregnant woman I hadn't met before.

"Looks like Artie loves it," I gestured to the wad of blankets and the heavy tank of fluorocarbon underneath them. "We'll get out of your hair."

Erikson nodded and pressed the wall to release the sliding compartment that held the diaper disposers.

I grabbed the stroller's handles and pushed it out of the room. Chanda walked next to me, her hand over one of mine grabbing it as hard as she had when she'd given birth.

The stroller wobbled under the weight of the tank since it was a tad heavier than the baby that this stroller was supposed to carry. But at least I knew it wasn't going to burst out in tears drawing more attention to us.

***

The cell was already hot since we were on the side of the dome that faced the evening sun. My jumpsuit was rolled down to my waist and I already had wet stains under the arms of my t-shirt.

I was looking forward to taking a cold shower in the bathing compartment that popped up out of the floor. Smelling the sweet shampoo in my wet hair would be a nice break from this room's hot musk. And then there was dinner. I didn't care what we were having, I longed for the taste of anything savory and filling.

But first I had to finish up this supercharging job. Dozens of metal and plastic pipes and ran to and from behind the segment of the LED wall I'd removed. The disconnected panel lay on the floor leaning against the new stroller. The rest of the LED walls were playing an image of a bright green forest at sunset.

The tank of extra fluorocarbon was plumbed into the recharging port with a foot-long bendable plastic pipe. Hooking it in had been easy enough, the manual was clear on the steps for that. Now it was only a matter of time before the cooling utility took advantage of the extra fluorocarbon and the vents of this cell started blowing ice cold air.

What the manual didn't go over was how to stash the tank in an inconspicuous manner so I could put the paneling back on. I'd almost given up. A segment of dead cells would be a worthy price to pay for a good night's sleep.

Chanda, who'd shed the lab coat and long clothes for some light-weight gym shorts and shirt, was pacing nervously back and forth in the mostly empty room.

Both the table and bed were stored away in the floor. That didn't keep the room from being cluttered with Artie's stuff. Her toys and equipment weren't the only thing cluttering the room anymore. I had a pile of wrenches, pliers, and screwdrivers scattered around the floor.

Artie herself was quietly sleeping in the crib. Hopefully, she wouldn't be the only one getting a decent night's rest. I was exhausted between today's big heist and last night's fitful and sweaty sleep.

"And we're supposed to break into the storeroom every month?" Chanda asked, rhetorically. It was the fourth time I'd heard that question. She wasn't looking forward to the chore. I thought it a worthy price to pay for the comfort of my girls.

"Only until the summer months on this planet end. And next year we'll be sure to get a coolant pump earlier. Or we'll move to an interior room," I said. I lifted the tank up once more, still heavy with the fluorocarbon, and tried to jam it into a gap I found.

It clinked against the metal pipes and I didn't want to push any harder for fear of damaging an already strained cooling utility.

The digital chime of a visitor at our cell door startled all three of us. Chanda and I looked at each other in silent nervousness. Artie began to wail.

I scrambled to put the panel back on the wall, but it wouldn't fit with the hose coming out.

"Who is it?" I asked.

"Erikson," Chanda replied.

I gave up on the paneling, we couldn't leave him waiting for long. If he was suspicious of us any delay would just be more evidence.

I decided to put the tank back in the stroller. Then I covered it with a few of Artie's stuffed animals. I covered the paneling with all the blankets that Chanda had checked out, plus a few more that Artie had spit up on over the past few weeks.

Erikson rang the cell's doorbell again.

Artie was infuriated.

I looked at my sloppy job, it wouldn't fool anyone under close inspection. But we'd just have to make sure Erikson didn't do a close inspection.

"Open the door. We'll figure it out," I said to Chanda as I picked up Artie to comfort her.

Chanda walked to the door slowly. She pressed the handle and the door slid open fitting itself into its neat little pocket in the doorframe.

"Quartermaster Erikson," she greeted him cheerily. "How can we help you?"

Erikson stepped into the room under a canopy of trees that were displayed on the LED wall.

"I saw you at the storeroom today," he said, "but didn't see that you'd logged your entry."

"Oh dear," Chanda said. "What could've caused that?"

"I'm not sure I'm having some techs investigate it. What all did you check out?" he pulled out a small tablet to mark down what we'd taken.

"Just the stroller, and a few blankets," Chanda said.

"Well, I'll need the serial number of the stroller and know exactly how many blankets," he said walking across the room towards the stroller and the loosely mounted paneling.

"Oh, you don't want to touch those," I said to him once he got closer to them. Artie was still screaming in my arms. She was so close to my BO, I couldn't blame her.

"The reason we've needed so many is because little Artie is not agreeing with the bits of solid food, we've started to give her. Blows chunks like a drunkard every evening."

Quartermaster Erikson hesitantly laughed at my comment but was determined to get to the blankets and stroller.

As if Artie was trying to help sell my story she spat up on the shoulder of my t-shirt. Just a little bit of green goop, nothing I hadn't seen before as a mother. I rocked her up and down with a few bounces. That seemed to quell her a little bit.

The quartermaster on the other hand backed away from the paneling more uncomfortable than the baby.

"I'll count out which blankets are new along with their color," I assured him. "And get that serial number off the stroller tonight."

"That would be very helpful. And in the future make sure that your checkouts are logged." Erikson headed towards the door.

"Thanks for checking up on us," Chanda said in a tone that, to me, conveyed this should've been a message, not a house call.

"And then there was one more thing I wanted to discuss," Erikson said standing under the arc of digital trees.

If Artie hadn't been crying my gulp would've endlessly echoed off the smooth walls of the square cell.

"I was able to find an older coolant pump," Erikson said. "It needed some repairs but the techs got it working again. I didn't want to promise anything earlier because...well the only thing worse than a stingy quartermaster is one that overpromises and underdelivers."

He dragged in a large coolant pump from the hallway outside. It was a little taller than his waist and thicker than I expected.

"It's pretty cool in here right now," he remarked.

I hadn't noticed the change in temperature since I was nervously sweating about his arrival.

"Oh, I'm sure that will change soon," I said. Hoping it wouldn't.

"Well let me know if you have any issues with it," he said. "Otherwise enjoy your evening."

"You too Erikson," Chanda said leading him to the door. When it slid shut behind him, she looked at me with a smile I hadn't seen since I proposed to her.

"I'm glad it's going to be so cool in here because I'm sweating bullets," Chanda said.

Artie quelled down once our intruder was gone. I looked at her and gave her a tiny smile. Her big baby cheeks were like rosy bubbles and her tiny lips were puckered clueless of what we'd just risked for her comfort. For our comfort.

"It's a good thing your mommy got you all those blankets," I said, "because we're going to be cold tonight."

The coolant utility was humming away determined to make use of the extra fluorocarbon we'd connected to it. I wandered around the small room for a moment until I found where the hidden vents were blowing ice-cold air.

Artie giggled at the cold air that hit her in the face. I gave little Artie a kiss because she looked so cute laughing.

I turned my back to shield her from it and to soak up as much of the cold air as I could. This was almost better than a shower.

Chanda, always a little cooler than me hence why I married her, slid out the panel of the wall that was her wardrobe. She thumbed through it looking for a sweater. She picked out a thick one, one that I was pretty sure had once been mine. It didn't matter, I had no plans to wear anything thicker than a T-shirt tonight, thanks to the environment of this room turning into something pleasant.

Just like we would turn the environment of the desert planet on the other side of the cell's wall. There were still plenty of terraforming efforts to be done to make this planet a comfortable place to live. But I'd done a pretty good job setting up this room to be a chilly paradise.

I had no doubt that this planet would become a paradise too, for our daughter, her siblings, and any other ancestors they chose to have. I'd make sure the planet provided a comfortable future for Artie, no matter what. Because moving here was not a miscalculation.

Supper With Kraken-folk

Synthetic dirt covered the ground of the room. It was a half-hearted replica of the soil found in the Rocky Mountain Archipelagos where Tankel grew up. This ground was similar to his most recent home. Except there, most of the decorations were real, even if the depths of the sea wore them down.

Four thick glass walls surrounded him and the other humans and kept the water around them at bay. An air purifier hummed away incessantly in a corner, a sound he was used to by now.

Inside the walls sat a house in the old suburban style, two stories with large windows that gave anyone outside the house a clear view of what the humans were doing. A tree sat in front of the house, its polystyrene apples picked off by some previous tenant and littered near the plastic trunk.

A dozen people were dropped off with him this morning. A few of them cried, unable to come to terms with their new situation. No one in his transport batch spoke English, and he felt strange seeing human faces and unable to talk to them.

Tankel walked up to the house. The front door lacked a latch, so it swayed lazily as he passed through. A few people sat at the dining room table also speaking in a language he didn't understand. They greeted him politely, and he waved with a smile. The area was two stories tall, but there was no way to get to the second-floor mezzanine. The kraken-folk designer hadn't grasped, or cared, that humans couldn't naturally move vertically like them.

He found the kitchen and pulled on the fridge door. As a kid on the Rocky Mountain islands, he remembered getting in trouble for standing in front of the town's fridge on hot summer days. This fridge door stayed shut since the machine was merely a model. He could see where the refrigerator was sculpted away from the wall and cabinets.

"Feeding time is in a few hours," a man with black hair said. He was sitting at a bar stool, rolling an apple up his arm, then popping his elbow to make it bounce into his hand. "They feed you before dropping you off?"

"No," Tankel replied as he checked a few drawers and cabinets. Each one was merely decorative. He levered himself up onto the counter to take a seat. It looked as comfortable as the plastic stool his acquaintance sat on. "How long have you been here?"

"A few weeks. I'm Nagji." He caught the apple in his hand and reached out his other to shake across the bar.

"Tankel," he replied.

"We don't get a lot of people from the Americas here. How'd you get caught?"

"I was sailing to the Appalachian Islands. A kraken-folk grabbed my ship and pulled us down. I've spent the past few years alone with a little kraken-folk poking at my tank with his little suction cups."

"Those are the worst," he shook his head.

Tankel shrugged. "I had an actual weight bench which gave me something to do. And regular meals of raw fish. Although I'd kill for a salad or toast."

"Best they do here is some seaweed slop."

Seaweed reminded Tankel of his grandfather. The man's breath was always heavy with the salty stuff as he told of times when the small islands were mountains, and the octopuses would fit in a bucket. Everyone knew what caused the flooding; they'd known it would happen for generations. But high tides and storms wiped out the infrastructure that could help humanity figure out why the kraken-folk grew in size and intelligence. Tankel grew up hearing all the legends used to explain the phenomenon. Some claimed coastal nuclear reactors mutated them, or an abundance of ocean gave them space to evolve. His grandfather had the crazy idea that the kraken-folk were always this smart; they just didn't live long enough to use it.

"I get the impression this isn't a museum," Tankel eventually said after staring out the window at the rocky nests that littered the floor around their glass room. A pair of octopuses nestled into rocks and turned their heads toward the human habitat.

"No, not quite," Nagji replied, tossing the apple towards Tankel. "You want to play catch in the yard? I'm feeling lucky."

"I'm feeling less lucky by the second. And I don't think I'll enjoy my stay here." Tankel looked at the apple. It was painted a single shade of red lacking the yellow and orange streaks he expected from the fruit.

"I haven't." Nagji's tone was flat.

"You've been here a while... any point in putting off the inevitable?"

"Everyone gets caught eventually."

"I was never one to procrastinate," Tankel said with a shrug. He left the kitchen, and Nagji followed. A dozen people flooded through the door as some mechanism whirled to life outside.

"I liked my time with the little kraken-folk, though," Tankel continued. "It beat life on the island where we worked the ground for food and built houses out of scraps. Especially when those scraps are torn apart during every storm."

Tankel tossed the apple to Nagji, who stood under the tree. A few people sat in the yard shouting denials or bargains at the machine in the sky.

The machine lowered a glass cup down and into the dirt behind Tankel, and he fell in as the synthetic ground slid out from under his feet. The faux apple landed near him while Nagji leaned against the tree's trunk for protection.

The cup sealed itself with Tankel inside, and he climbed to his feet on the shifting ground. A few more mechanisms hissed and latched into place, and the glass moved through the water. His little environment had separated from the larger habitat.

The cup nestled into the center of the kraken-folk's nest, and the giant beasts inspected him. Their large suction cups squished onto the glass. Tankel flailed around in the dirt as they chirped at each other. Then a needle with gas entered the ceiling of the cup. It smelled noxious, and Tankel coughed, trying to get the fumes out of his lungs. Water rushed in, and the air bubble he stood in floated away as he helplessly swam through the cloud of fake dirt.

A tentacle grabbed him and dragged him under the beast's bulbous head. Tankel instinctually wrestled against the beast's grasp to no avail. Finally, the tentacle shoved him into the opening where the eight tentacles met.

Unable to hold his breath any longer, he gasped in shock and swallowed salty water. The walls of the beast's gullet crushed him as he suffocated to death.

"It kicks going down," the kraken-folk said.

"Don't worry, that's just a reflex," the other replied before ordering another glass of fresh human.

Outskirts of the Family

Jane and Angi couldn't find a single picture of Jane's brother, Phil. He wasn't at her wedding, wasn't in any of the family vacation photos, and of course there was no luck on social media, the guy practically broke out in hives if you brought those platforms up.

Jane had composed family photos of a dozen other landmarks in their life but her twin wasn't in a single one. If she wasn't so confident he'd be here today she'd have given up hours ago.

The house smelled like cinnamon and sage. Donovan worked tirelessly in the kitchen basting the turkey every half hour in between other cooking chores like peeling potatoes and kneading the dough for the dinner rolls.

For Thanksgiving, the kitchen was Donovan's domain, but the rest of the small condo belonged to Jane, and she'd spent the past few weeks decorating it and rearranging furniture to accommodate the dozen family members that would soon be arriving for dinner. The table was extended to its full length. Cloth blue chairs and wooden black ones surrounded it. They were set in an alternating pattern that made the motley furniture look intentional.

The white tablecloth was clean, she'd be impressed if it made it through the day without a little red wine or cranberry sauce on it. A burnt orange runner cutting through the center, she'd picked that up last minute and was glad to be rid of the old green and red embroidered one, not quite the right color for the occasion.

A small kid's table was set off to the side for her niece and nephew. She'd set out a few coloring books and a fresh box of crayons. As a kid, she always hated going to relative's houses without anything to do. Now she hated that kids came to visit her and didn't look past their augmented reality unless it was to eat.

The smart walls were covered in a collage of family photos from the years scrolling past. Jane had scraped a few of them from social media. She pulled a couple others off the condo's hard drive. All in all, it was far better than any wallpaper she could've plastered up.

She'd had it running for the past few days enjoying being surrounded by her family. Looking forward to their visit.

Donovan had installed their smart home system a few years ago. It linked with the embedded neuro-processors that Jane, Donovan, and everyone else in the civilized world used for communication and day-to-day activities.

She hadn't found the smart home particularly useful. Her name was Angi, artificial neural generative intelligence, and she could take care of small tasks, playing music, decorating the walls, adjusting the thermostat. But the link to the neuro-processors was one-sided.

Until Donovan had found an update.

Now she found Angi inside her head, in the best possible ways. Adjusting the thermostat before Jane realized she was cold, changing songs to suit her mood.

And now Angi was helping her find a picture of her brother Phil in the house's database.

Not that either of them were having any luck.

"What does Phillip look like?" Angi asked. "Picture him in your head so I might know what to look for."

It wasn't the first time it had asked. For something that was in Jane's head and had terabytes of memory, this seemed like something that wouldn't be forgotten.

"Brown hair like me, blue eyes, but a darker blue than mine, almost royal blue. He's got my mom's nose. Small and buttony." Jane was always jealous of that. She'd inherited her father's large Italian hooked nose and even after 15 years of Donovan telling her it was cute she didn't believe him.

"Ok, I think I've got a photo of him at the wedding," Angi said throwing the image on the dining room wall that Jane faced.

Sure enough, there was Phil in the group photo of everyone on the bride's side. Donovan and Jane were in the center. Her parents were behind her, and her sister Nicole and her husband Clay stood behind

Donovan. Nicole held Patricia who was barely 8 months old. A dozen aunts and uncles, cousins, and close family friends surrounded the newlyweds.

And there was Philip, tiny nose, clean-shaven, in a suit like her father's, standing on the edge.

There were practically twenty people in this photo. It wasn't a surprise that Philip had slipped by unnoticed.

But why did he choose to stand on the outskirts of the family? He should be next to Nicole and their parents. Only Phil could explain that.

"Why wasn't this the first one we checked?" Jane asked, using her embedded neuro-processor to arrange the photo inside the collage. She found where to put it, nestled in with the other wedding photos. A great aunt and uncle were hidden behind a picture of the reception in order to put Phil, on the edge, center in the collage.

"There's no shortage of wedding photos to go through," Angi replied.

While rearranging the wedding part of the collage Jane found another version of the same group picture without Phil in it. With a flicking gesture, more to help her mind focus on the action than Angi, she trashed it.

"Now you know who you're looking for any luck?" Even a photo of him in the background would be acceptable.

And, as if Angi read her mind, a dozen more photos appeared on the wall. Most of them with Phil in the background. But there was one good one of Donovan and Phil taking shots together at the bachelor party. Jane had to fit in. If only to prove to Donovan that he had met Phil. It was no wonder Donovan denied meeting her brother, he was too drunk to remember it.

Once Angi knew what she was looking for Phil showed up everywhere. He was bundled up and almost unrecognizable in ski goggles and a scarf but his button nose, red from the chill, made it clear it was him.

In another great photo, he was dressed up in a skeleton costume, face painted white as bone. He was mock scaring Princess Patricia and her vampire brother Nate some countless Halloweens ago. Soon enough he was in just about every memorable family vacation and event Jane had displayed on the walls.

You'd almost believe he wasn't a recluse and a Luddite.

"Your mother has arrived," Angi said as Jane displayed the last of her brother's photos.

A second later the doorbell rang. Phil came by his technophobia honestly, Mom refused to adopt or trust much of anything invented after Jane went to college.

Jane shuffled down the hardwood stairs as fast as she could without slipping. Angi was already acting as a butler using the motors of the front door to swing it open. Donovan always joked their condo was like a haunted mansion, in ghostly activity and price.

"You can't come down and open the door for your own mother?" Jane's mom said as she hobbled inside.

For better or worse it seemed her mom's memory was doing alright today. That would thankfully cut down on uncomfortable confusion but meant the snide remarks would be attending in droves.

"Happy Thanksgiving to you too," Jane replied with a smile and kissed her mother. "And it's good to see you too Ash," Jane said offering the nurse a hand with the bags in their arms.

"Where's that strapping young husband of yours to carry me up these stairs?" Jane's mom asked.

It'd take more than one strapping young husband to get Mom up those stairs.

Jane offered her hand to help her mom up. "Donny can't lift much more than a book without throwing his back out these days."

Ash followed, with the watchful eye of a caregiver. They'd been with Mom since a little after Dad's death. Ash was practically family at this point. The younger sibling that Jane and Phil never had.

"Well I sure earned whatever delicious meal Donovan is cooking up in there," Mom said as she plopped herself on the couch, exhausted from the hike up the stairs.

"Glad to see you, Shirley," Donovan said slipping out of the kitchen to greet Jane's mother and giving her a quick peck on the cheek, knowing he'd catch hell from the old woman if he didn't greet her.

"Hey, look what I found," Jane said gesturing at the collage on the wall.

The picture of Donovan and Phillip at the bachelor party took up the entire wall as Angi anticipated what Jane wanted to show her husband.

Donovan looked shocked at the almost life-size version of his younger self throwing back a small glass of whiskey in a crowded and dimly lit bar.

"No way," Donovan said.

Jane could tell he wasn't surprised or delighted like her. This "no way" had the tone of an impending disagreement and subsequent argument. But that's what she got for marrying a lawyer.

"You going to argue with photo evidence?" Jane asked.

"Donovan you need to get the sweet potatoes in the oven now," Angi said. How anyone managed such a complex meal without the house keeping track of timetables was a mystery to Jane.

"It's just we took a three-row SUV to the bar, it was full with Mike, Chuck, me, Dan, Kyle, and the Johnson brothers. Where would Phillip fit?" Donovan asked.

Jane shrugged.

A second reminder about the sweet potatoes dragged Donovan back to the kitchen.

"You've done a lovely job decorating," Ash said after checking that everything was alright with Mom.

"Let me see these photos of Philip," Mom said.

Angi put a few up on the wall that Mom's couch was facing.

"He never visits," Mom added in the same frustrated but resigned tone she remarked about all her children not coming out to see her enough. If it was up to her Ash would be replaced by one, if not all three, of her children.

"He'll be here today," Jane said. She'd hounded him for months to make sure he was free.

"He's not eating enough either, always had trouble putting on weight after he was sick as a baby."

The group wedding photo came up. Mom went on about some of the other people in the photo, her aunts and sister, what they were doing and what they should be doing.

"She has this photo framed in the living room of her apartment," Ash said. "But you're brother's not in it."

"No, we just found it today," Jane said.

"Well, I'm sure she'd like it, print one out for her if you don't mind. Do you have any of just him?"

Angi produced a still portrait of Philip in the red and gold graduation garb of Jane's alumni: Arizona Tech.

"Oh my!" Mom said as if she was seeing a ghost. "He looks so handsome," the words came out between tears.

"I'm surprised this isn't hanging up with you and Nicole's graduation photos," Ash said in a hushed tone to Jane.

"Phillip didn't go to Tech," Jane said confused about how this photo, which looked similar to her graduation photo, existed. "Never graduated from any college. Didn't need a *traditional* education. Nature would teach him everything he needed to know."

"There's also this photo of him fishing with your dad," Angi said replacing the strange graduation photo with a photo of Phillip holding a largemouth bass the size of his chest. Their father stood next to him with a slightly smaller one that looked the same size only because his arm was extended to get the fish closer to the camera.

The two men were standing in a square flat bottom boat, the old Boston Whaler. Her dad had a mustache, instead of the beard he wore when they were kids. It was strange to Jane because she was pretty sure the beard disappeared around the same time as the boat. Replaced with a sparkly bottomed bass boat. And that all happened before she went to college because her mom had joked too many times that he'd spent Jane's college fund on the damn thing.

But here was Philip a grown man, even if he was as lean as a high schooler, fishing with his father.

"Your dad always wanted to take Phillip fishing," Mom said her eyes still watering a little bit.

Jane would have to ask Philip when he got here when this photo was taken. Surely he'd remember catching a bass this big.

"Please, print her off as many of these as you have," Ash said. "Old photos like this help her. And she never talks about your brother."

No one in the family ever seemed to want to talk about Phillip. Ever since she was a kid, she'd tattle on Phillip and no one would listen. She'd tell her sister Nicole about what back country shenanigans he was into, or how getting a sailing license was going and Nicole would change the subject.

"Jane," Angi said and it was on the private bone-conductive communication channel that Angi used when Donovan was asleep or he was busy with a phone call of his own. "Your brother just sent a message that he won't be able to make it today."

Jane growled in frustration. Ash looked at her, but her mother ignored it still looking at the photo of her son plastered up on the wall. Jane excused herself to the upstairs office.

Shelves of thick law books covered one wall. A large corner desk that Donovan used took up most of the rest of the room. The small desk that Jane rarely used had a printer on it. And Angi, ever anticipating, had already printed off the wedding photo with Philip in it.

"What's Phil's excuse for not coming?" Jane asked. "I told him I'd hunt him down in whatever backwoods cabin he's staying in and drag him out here."

"A family emergency came up," Angi replied.

"Family? Emergency? Who's he got to take care of that isn't going to be in this room today?! Call him."

A ring played in her ear as Jane looked at the wedding photo. Ringing her skinny brother's neck wouldn't be too hard.

An automated voicemail came up, Jane left a nasty and frustrated message. If Phillip turned up dead today this would probably convince the jury she was behind it.

And if he didn't call her back the jury would be right.

"Nicole and her family are here," Angi announced over the speakers of the house. The computer didn't need to announce it because Nate and Patricia stomped up the stairs quickly.

The two kids, bounded around the room giving everyone hugs and kisses before their parents even made it up the stairs. Nicole and Clay were having some argument about the drive down here but smiled graciously at everyone once they entered the room.

"We finished saying hi to everyone? Can I have my game back?" Nate asked.

"After dinner," Clay replied. He pointed to the kid's table where Jane had set out some crayons and coloring books. "Do something analog for a bit."

Nicole finished hugging their mom and walked up to Jane. "Here's the salad and some Rice-A-Roni. I hope Donovan's not offended, it's about the only thing that satisfies Nate's eight-year-old palate."

"No worries," Jane replied. "No one's going to pick a fight on Thanksgiving."

Well, someone might, but that's why Nicole wasn't hosting this year.

"Who's the guy fishing with dad?" Nicole asked gesturing at the image taking up most of the living room wall. She handed the salad and casserole dish to Clay who was going to the kitchen to see if Donovan needed help, or maybe he just wanted out of the busy living room.

"That's Philip," Jane said to her sister trying not to sound like she was insulting the woman's intelligence. "We found some old photos of him today. Been showing them to mom."

Nicole's face looked like an Arizona monsoon had swept in. "You're not serious," Nicole said.

"Yeah, it's remarkable. I thought he'd sworn off cameras and photos but we've got half a dozen decent ones."

"This is a cruel joke to play on mother," Nicole said. "And on Thanksgiving. Take them down!"

Angi did as it was told and the pictures of Phillip disappeared from the walls, even in the collage, replaced by an earlier version of the wallpaper.

"Hey, what gives?" Jane asked.

But her sister was on the couch cooing soft reassurance to their mother who was doing her best to hide her tears.

Nicole had been here less than five minutes and had already started a fight. And there was no doubt the woman would find a way to make it Jane's fault.

Ash, confused, joined Nicole by Mom's side. Nicole took the relief and marched back over to Jane.

"What were you thinking?" Nicole asked, still furious.

"What's going on with you?"

"You never let it go. It was cute when you were five and he was an imaginary friend but I thought you'd dropped it."

"Phillip, *our brother*, is not my imaginary friend!"

"You're right he's not imaginary," Nicole conceded. "Our brother Phillip has been dead since you were three."

"No. There are pictures. I remember him."

"*I remember*," Nicole sneered. "I remember staying with you at grandma's while mom and dad went back and forth to the hospital. I remember the funeral, the tiny casket, the fights that Mom and Dad had afterward. Counseling that I went to and you got out of because Mom didn't want you out of her sights."

Jane pulled out a chair from the dining room and fell back into it dazed. This was the most her sister had talked about Phillip in years, and it was just more lies and slander.

"No. Mom remembered him today."

"Mom thinks dad's at the corner station most days," Nicole said. "I'm more worried about you. You're around the same age that Mom was when Dad first notices small lapses in her memory."

Well at least this was familiar: Nicole the hypochondriac. Always anxious about some disease or another. Always worried Clay was going to have a heart attack. The woman hadn't missed a well-woman exam in 25 years. She was convinced one of her babies would get leukemia or some other awful disease. Her latest concern was Patricia getting mono from a boy even though she was hardly a teenager. Of course, Nicole would blame Jane's memory.

"But Angi found these pictures today. Proof that he's alive and doing well. Proof that I'm not imagining him."

They were twins, losing him would be like losing part of herself. She'd remember that. She hadn't lost him. She was connected to him in the way only twins could be connected. Better than any technology could connect them. No matter what backwoods cabin he was living in. Or how far off shore he'd sailed she could feel him and knew he was enjoying himself.

"Angi," Nicole said with her most motherly scold. "Where did these photos come from?"

"Using the images of Jane's memory I reconstructed Philip and put him in a few photos. I knew it was important to Jane to have Phillip present today. These photos were the best I could do."

"There ya go," Nicole said throwing her hands up in the air. "AI ruins yet another holiday!"

"Phillip visited me in college. He was at my wedding! Did Halloween with the kids when they were young." Jane felt the harvest-colored room spin around her.

"He messaged me today," Jane added. "he said he wouldn't make it but I called him!" Clearly it wasn't Jane's mind that was slipping, it was her *older* sister.

"I'm sorry Jane," Angi said, "I simulated the call and message."

"But I hounded him for weeks to come today!" Jane's shouting had brought both Donovan and Clay into the room from the Kitchen.

"My records have no outgoing calls or messages to anyone named Phillip, or anyone connected as your brother," Angi said.

"Why?" Jane said. "Why lie? Why hallucinate these memories for me?"

"Because to you Jane, he isn't a hallucination," Angi said. "These pictures are how you genuinely remember these events. As far as your mind is concerned Phillip attended all these key moments of your life and more."

"Monday morning we're taking you to get a CAT scan," Nicole said. "You could have a tum–"

"Nicole, leave your sister alone," their mother said in the tone all mothers use to cut off bickering.

"Of course, you come to her side," Nicole, also a mother of two, snapped back. And an age-old fight was revived between the two women.

Jane wandered out of the living room, up the stairs, and into the office. She wanted to be alone, and mourn the loss of her brother in peace.

At least she thought she'd be alone in the office.

A man, lanky as a high schooler, leaned on Jane's small desk. He held a small piece of paper in his hands.

His royal blue eyes were like the deep ocean waves he spent years learning to sail. His button nose looked just like their mother's. His smile was warm and comforting like their father's.

"I knew you would make it," Jane said.

"Wouldn't miss it for the world, sis."

"They miss you out there," Jane said. But she knew he wouldn't be leaving the office. "No one's seen you in a while."

"I miss them too," Phillip said looking at the wedding photo. The one with everyone in it, including him. "Tell them I said hello."

He pressed the photo firmly into Jane's hand. His bony fingers were rigid and cold like a bass coming out of a cooler.

Jane looked at the photo. Looked at her clean-shaven twin brother grinning from ear to ear full of pride for his sister.

But why did he choose to stand on the outskirts of the family? He should be next to Nicole and their parents. Only Phil could explain that.

But Jane figured it was because that was as close as he could ever get to the family.

The Djinn-erator

"Genies are only ever found in ancient lamps," Caitlyn Voglefonte explained to her husband. "Which is why I figured if I'd age some lamps with my chronon field where time runs faster than out here."

"Sure," Samuel replied, "and we're just assuming that genies are an actual thing that exists?" He had to change his perspective on a lot of things lately, and it was uncomfortable for him.

The couple stood in their basement workshop. It'd once been an even split of Samuel's woodworking tools and Caitlyn's electronic and manufacturing equipment. Unlike her, he didn't want engineering to be his hobby but Caitlyn couldn't get enough of it. Once he conceded space for her CNC mill she'd crept further and further into his side of the shop with more new tools. All that extra equipment led to her recent discovery. The chronon field one, not the genie one. He was still unsure about the genies.

Caitlyn reached into the subspace portal with a pair of metal tongs. If she put her bare hands in it they would age, wrinkle, and eventually decay in a matter of minutes. She pulled out an LED camping lantern, the plastic looked brand new, despite having aged a few hundred years in the chronon field.

"Isn't it supposed to be an oil lantern?" Samuel asked.

"Why? Because that's what the stories always say?"

Samuel nodded then rolled his eyes in resignation. If Caitlyn looked at the world like everyone else she wouldn't have bastardized the newly published warp drive research into a chronon field like this. Which is what he loved about her.

"It was only an oil lamp because genies like light sources and oil lamps lasted the longest. Turns out the Djinn aren't picky about the light source as long as it's portable."

"That's a funny line to draw."

"People like what they like. No one gives you a hard time for wearing sunglasses even when it's cloudy."

"It could– never mind. What are we supposed to do?" He knew the answer but felt silly saying it and was done taking things for granted.

"I just have to rub it," she started polishing the smooth plastic. Nothing happened for a minute but Caitlyn's face was relaxed, as sure the genie would appear as Galileo was in the Earth's orbit.

It took longer than Samuel expected but eventually, the air around the lamp got hazy. It wasn't quite like a cloud of smoke although he didn't blame writers and poets for using the metaphor as shorthand.

To him, it looked like the refraction of a straw in a cup of water. The effect repeated dozens of times with less than a centimeter distance between them and it was localized around the lamp in half a meter in every direction. Then a greenish filter tinted the area, increased in opacity, and transformed into a solid being before his eyes.

Samuel groaned. Of course, genies were real. Why did he ever doubt her?

"If it would make you feel better we could refer to it as a multidimensional alien that is predisposed to granting requests by the beings who contact it through portable light sources," Caitlyn offered.

"No. Genie is fine. But aren't they known for double-crossing people who wish on things?"

Samuel looked at the being in front of him. It was humanoid in shape, and he wondered if the genie picked the shape as a preference, because of evolution, or for Samuel's comfort. Its skin was green like a dill pickle. Instead of rippling muscles, it wore long robes that flowed with the straw in water refraction effect. It made him nauseous to look at it for too long. Caitlyn didn't mind. She was smiling comfortably, pleased with her discovery.

"Wait, can you understand us?" Samuel asked.

"Yes," a voice replied. It didn't shake his chest like a subwoofer, but the words reverberated in his mind. Like deja vu but in a shorter increment of time.

"We could ask so many questions about life, the universe, and everything! Like where it comes from or how many other life forms are out there in the cosmos?"

"Is that your wish?" the genie said looking at Caitlyn.

"No," Caitlyn replied. "I wish we had some pizzas."

"Very well." The genie disappeared from in front of them with a snap. For an instant, it felt to Samuel that nothing stood in the space in front of him and that nothing was dragging him in like the current of a rushing river.

"Pizza!?" Samuel said when the room returned to feeling normal.

"Of course! You *really* wanted me to have him explain cosmos-level problems to us? That's a quick way to go insane!"

"Well, sure we'd have to do some setup first. But don't we get three wishes?"

"Number of wishes is determined by the time spent in the djinn-er-ator."

Samuel chuckled at her device's name. "Okay, but where's the pizza."

The doorbell rang in response.

"Why didn't you wish for something like world peace?" Samuel said as they went to see who was at the door. "Or more money for your research? Or for the kitchen to be clean?"

Caitlyn opened the door. A pizza delivery driver stood in front of them with two pizzas and a bottle of cola.

"Do I owe you anything?" Caitlyn asked as she took the pizzas from him.

"Nope it was paid for on the app," the driver replied.

Samuel closed the door behind her as she set the pizzas on the dinner table. She examined them and then pointed to the label. "The driver delivered it to White Hart *Street* instead of White Hart *Court*."

"Ok, so the genie manipulates events to make the things you wish to appear?"

"Which is why my wish for world peace and research funding hasn't come through yet."

"You already made those wishes?"

"Of course!" Caitlyn said with a smile. "And you were already doing dishes in the kitchen so I didn't need to waste a wish on that."

Freeze-dried Preserves

Theta Lorimer Harding never quite knew every detail about what her ship was delivering. She didn't even know where it was going until the last waypoint buoy was reached. And even when the container was delivered she often never learned the details about her deliveries. It bothered her. She was shocked it didn't bother more

people. But she knew whatever she was delivering was real and important. And that made the darkness bearable.

But it didn't make the hurry-up-and-wait aspect of her job any
better. She waited two days on Hebron for the cargo container to
finish getting loaded. She was now waiting in subspace headed as fast as
the ship could go to get to the next buoy. And Theta Harding had no
doubt that there would also be waiting once she arrived at the Gamma
ship to deliver the cargo.

Theta Harding opened her eyes to see her blurry reflection on the
silver paneling of the domed ceiling. The sharp aroma of cleaning
supplies made it clear that the scrubbots had just completed their pass
through the room. Her stomach ached and she looked forward to the
savory freeze-dried chili that was about to be her dinner.

Three big soft cushions of the round table chair pressed into her
back and shoulders. The strap around her sternum kept her in place
now that the ship was done accelerating into subspace. They would
travel in the no-man's land that was subspace for a few hours to get to
the next buoy which would provide further directions. An even bigger
rounder cushion supported her butt, and the seatbelt around her waist
pressed her into that. All the cushions were shaped like lily pads and
were just as dark green as the foliage. It was nearly the only pop of color
in the room.

The neon green gel of the interface helmet was the other pop
of color. The helmet-shaped headrest that surrounded her head like
horse blinders had a thick film of neon green gel that interfaced her
mind with the navigation of the ship. That was its stated purpose.
Its secondary purpose was to let the six crew members explore the
infinite virtual world of the Local Area Metaverse. And that might
be its most important purpose, since without the distraction crew

members would be inclined to explore the small delivery ship and poke at electronics that had no business being poked at.

Currently, her scalp and hair were pressed against the sticky gel. Her hair would come clean easy enough in the shower, especially now that she had it cut pixie short. But it'd take a week out of the gel to clear it from her ears. Of course, she wouldn't have to clean it off as often if she didn't feel the need to leave the LAM multiple times each delivery.

The cockpit, although it had no windows or navigational displays, was designed to be barren and boring. It was circular with a few metal handrails running around the perimeter. These handrails always reminded Theta Harding of a fence she saw at a zoo as a girl.

She'd wanted to climb over the wall at the zoo, and she wanted to go past the handrails as well. Even if what waited for her on the other side was a few lions, or in this case, the vacuum of space.

She wasn't suicidal. That's why she was in the delivery corps instead of a metal-clad epsilon berserker fighting on the front line of some alien war. She wanted over the railing, out of this small cockpit, so that she might experience something new, something real, something that wasn't an illusion of synapses firing to create an elaborate fantasy in her head.

Which was also the reason she constantly disengaged from the LAM.

Theta Harding stood up from the chair and slicked back her hair using the residual gel to hold it in place. She wiggled a pinky finger into one ear, then another but only got a few globs of the green gel out. Unfortunately, she pushed just as much back into her ear canal. It felt like having water in her ear, something that never happened when swimming in the metaverse pools or oceans. And because of that the sensation wasn't unpleasant.

Theta Harding unlatched the buckle around her chest, then around her waist. She floated away from the pads slowly. She kicked off towards the metal railing that seemed to cage her in.

Various lockers and cabinets filled the space between the two railings. There were six coffin-sized lockers that held the thetas' personal items. A few had emergency medical supplies or repair equipment. Stuff Harding and the others hoped they'd never need to use. And the biggest held six spacesuits. Suits that they'd certainly never use despite spending most of their navigation time on the exterior surface of the ship.

Her bare feet hooked around the lower railing and the cold metal sent a shiver up her spine that flashed her into bright wakefulness. The LAM was like a dream and getting out of it was similar to waking up. Sometimes like waking up with a hangover, but waking up nonetheless.

The cockpit was chilly. The thin army green linen jumpsuit she wore did little to hold her body's heat in. But that was okay. Bodies ran hot in the LAM anyway, and the crispness of reality was a nice prod to remind her that this was real.

Slowly she shuffled sixty degrees around the room to access the food vendor. Behind her Theta Frangos was strapped into his green chair his eyes shut but moving quickly under his eyelids. He was remarkably thin as if a quick turn might snap him in two like a twig. She'd only ever palaved with him in the LAM and she didn't know when, or by his look if, he ate.

She could spend more time in the LAM like him. She might even lose a few pounds if she did. But neither of those were important, interesting, or necessary in her opinion.

The food vendor offered up a silver package in its metallic claw. It had a plain white label on the front that said Chili, along with a few serial numbers and barcodes that meant more to the fleet's chefs and robots than Harding.

In the gravity well there might be a delicious picture of what the meal would look like in a nice bright red bowl—everything in the well was bright red since it got people's attention. The Alfavito Fleet had no need to sell you illusions like that. It'd look like slop in the well and on the float.

Theta Harding gently peeled the seal off the top and dispensed hot water from a tube next to the food dispenser. She zipped it closed and let the food rehydrate. As the food came back to life so did Theta Kunle and Theta Thal. They were across the room, their backs to Harding. All the round table chairs had their backs to each other so that wires could feed down from the helmets into the center of the room's floor.

Theta Thal went straight for the head likely eager to wash the gel off their long blonde hair, coming out of the LAM was new to them. Theta Kunle had kinky black hair cropped close to his scalp and the bits of neon green gel were hardly noticeable. He floated towards Theta Harding with a light and energetic wave.

"Any thoughts about what to do about it?" Kunle asked. He was always quick to get to the point, the tiredness of LAM never seemed to affect him.

"Was too busy with the subspace calcs to give it much thought," Harding replied as Kunle got his own meal ready. In truth, the delivery's contents, and their strange noises, had hardly crossed her mind.

She massaged the chili making sure that the hot water made its way into every nook and cranny of the dehydrated meal. She didn't want to bite anything still crispy and dehydrated as she ate. The silver packaging of the food was supposed to keep the heat in but the package was still warm on her fingertips.

"You want to eat in here or out there?" Kunle asked gesturing at the door to the spine of the ship. It was the only other hatch in the cockpit aside from the head. And it should've been used significantly less often than the head but Harding had never found that to be true on any of the Theta ships.

"Out there's fine," Harding said grabbing a spoon and stuffing it, and the warm package of chili, into her jumpsuit. Her undershirt did little to keep the warmth of the food off her skin and it was a nice adversary to the chill of the cockpit.

The hatch that led to the spine of the ship was circular and exactly two meters in diameter—the length everything in the ship broke down to so that it could pass through hatches like this. A circular wheel in the center helped her disengage the dog clips around the edge that sealed the atmosphere of the cockpit from the spine. Now that they were in subspace they could relax their defensive posture and travel between the two compartments.

The entire ship, when it wasn't carrying massive cargo containers six times as big as it, was shaped like the carcass of a wooly mammoth. It had the round bulbous head that was the silver cockpit, and a rectangular spine marginally bigger than a human. The spine led to a small engine room which connected to the sleek tapered engines. Along the spine's exterior were four spidery legs on each side that locked onto the top of cargo containers that needed to be delivered across the galaxy to fleet outposts and occasionally war zones.

The spine was typically empty except for ladder rungs that made getting to the engine room, or the cargo, easier. None of the thetas were bold enough to touch the engine room, even Harding. But she was more than willing to make herself comfortable in the fairly empty spine.

Right now three hammocks hung from the footholds and hand-holds of the spine. They were held in place with heavy-duty carabiners and thick cords that could handle a few hundred kilonewtons of force. Force these hammocks would never see while floating in space. They wafted around like loose sails under a light breeze. The vibrations of the ship's engines and the air vents made small waves across the tropical warm colored hammocks.

The hammocks belonged to Harding, she'd picked one up on leave in an archipelago planet outpost a few years back and then two more when she realized hanging them in the spine was a lot more fun with friends.

She kicked off from the circular opening that led into the spine and aimed for the hammock closest to the engine room. It was fun to float past and try to dodge the soft fabric of the other two hammocks.

When she got closer to hers she kicked to twist herself in the air landing with her back in the hammock. Years ago she'd landed with her front in the hammock while holding a meal and getting the chili out of her jumpsuit was almost worse than getting the gel out of long hair.

Without gravity there wasn't much to keep you in the hammock, that was the great flaw of seating on the float. So much like the round table chairs Harding had installed ankle straps and a waist belt into the cloth of the hammock. Sure, floating in a hammock wasn't significantly different than floating without one but the warm colors they brought to the dingy grey walls of the spine were a nice escape. Plus the feeling of the soft synthetic cloth of the hammock was comforting even when compared to the thick cushioned lily pads of the round table chairs.

Harding got situated and went to town on the chili as the other two thetas wandered in and did the same. Most of the time the hiss of air vents and the theta's slow conversations filled the echoing chamber of the spine. But today they were often interrupted by the groans of whatever cargo they were carrying. The loud lethargic noise traveled in the form of vibrations from the cargo container through the spidery legs and the walls of the spine. At first, it was creepy, the sound seemed to emanate from every surface in the room. But now it was just frustrating.

Frustrating that they were interrupted and that they didn't know what was making the sound.

"It's not an animal," Theta Thal said between bites of jerk chicken that was far too spicy for Harding. "Transport of living creatures would require more fail-safes than the cargo containers have. Manifest for this container says it's mostly food for the Octocentenary celebration of the fleet. Mostly preserves, pickled vegetables, anything that lasts a while without being freeze-dried. Can't hold that at vacuum because the water will boil to vapor and freeze."

"It sounds so organic though," Kunle said, quite literally bouncing off the wall. He'd finished his meal quickly like he did just about everything.

"Intervals are too regular to be organic," Harding said. "It's a machine. And my question is should we go in and see if it needs to be fixed."

"Fix it?" Thal scoffed. "If we're transporting it then it's too complicated for us to fix."

Harding didn't say much to that. Instead, she scraped the last of the chili off the side of the bag and savored the last bite of the cooled food. Kunle floated threading the tight gap between her hammock and the wall.

"There's nothing saying we can't go and look." Harding poked a thumb at the hatch once she'd sealed her spoon into the now-empty bag of food. "If the deltas didn't want us in there then they'd mark it as top secret or hazardous."

"If the deltas wanted us in there they would've given us instructions on what we needed to do to maintain the cargo," Thal countered.

Harding could tell it was halfhearted. Which is why she wasn't surprised when she unstrapped from her hammock and saw Kunle already undoing the manual dog clips with a pipe to give him extra leverage. The last time this hatch was open was at least three deliveries ago.

There was a second hatch under the spine's hatch. It was a quicker entrance since that one was primarily electronic with a manual override. It could probably be triggered from the LAM if necessary. Most of the ship could be run from the LAM, yet another reason to never leave.

The cargo container was pitch black past the little bit of light the spine was able to throw own the short shaft between the two areas. The three thetas hesitantly floated inside and searched for a switch or something manual that would illuminate the container.

Yet another thing that could simply be controlled from the LAM.

Thal eventually found a switch that turned on the lights of the storage container. Slowly relay after relay flipped and the entire container was basked in sharp white light.

The container was big enough to hold some ships and occasionally the small theta delivery ships delivered replacement vehicles, although that was rare. More often the cargo was similar to what was held inside now.

Stacks of uniformly sized metal crates with rubbery bumps on the corners that protected them from falling damage and their raised and lowered surfaces that helped them lock into each for efficient and secure storage. Each of the six walls was covered with boxes. The stacks near the theta's entrance looked like stalactites hanging from the ceiling.

Harding shivered as she entered. Thal was right there was no life support and not much energy was spent on heating this room, it felt like a refrigerator inside. The room still smelled of diesel and petroleum, a scent left behind from the planet-side equipment that was used to load the container.

The diesel smell was familiar but still unique to Harding. Most of humanity's worlds hadn't progressed past late twentieth-century technology. They depended on technology that was simple enough that an average colonist, days away from other outposts, could maintain and repair the equipment. So there were specialists to fix non-quantum computers and maintain long-distance power lines and the generators that fueled them. Anything as advanced as the round table tech that this theta ship used was unrealistic to be maintained without entire companies of technicians. Densely populated city planets had these resources, and the kappa technicians of the Alfavito Fleet were constantly being deployed from one emergency to another, but most of humanity used and lived on something not much different from what their ancient ancestors experienced. Including Theta Harding who before joining the fleet hadn't seen anything more advanced than a touch screen hand terminal.

The groan of the cargo filled the entire container. It was so deep and strong that it shook Harding's ribcage. Instinctively she covered her ears, but it did little to block out the deep bellowing of the cargo.

Kunle was nonplused by the sound and pushed himself off of a crate to follow the noise. As quickly as it began it cut off. The room was silent except for the occasional thud of Kunle catching himself on a container. Harding and Thal followed as quickly as they could but Kunle was skilled moving on the float.

They followed mostly by the sound of Kunle bouncing off of crates. Then the groan happened and they couldn't hear anything but its deafening wails. Kunle didn't stop moving and he was eventually so far away in the three-dimensional maze of crates that it was impossible for the pair to follow him.

"Sweet stars around bless me," Kunle said. The statement echoed through the room but the bouncing didn't degrade the awe in his voice.

"Where are you?" Harding called back. And after a short game of Marco Polo, she found him floating in front of the largest mech suit Harding had ever seen.

The mech suit—which was humanoid in shape but unsettling boxy instead of the organically smooth shapes expected—was the size of a two-story building. Even though the thetas floated at its chest level it was difficult not to feel small and inadequate. The fact that Harding was clinging to the straps of some nearby crates made her feel even more like a child holding on for dear life.

Harding's first reaction was that surely this wasn't a piece of Alfavito equipment. The bright shades of purple, yellow, and red that were painted all over the boxy surface were a sure sign that someone far more creative than an Alfavito engineer was involved in its design. Not only was the metal surface colorful but it had decals on it like a teenager putting an irresponsible number of decals on their car. Everything from bright red flames to intricate circuit board patterns in black to characters in a script that Harding didn't recognize covered the arms, legs, and in one place the right breast, of the mech suit.

It groaned again and even Kunle had to cover his ears. Instinctively Harding squeezed her eyes shut as if that would stop her from hearing the sound. Her ears rang even after the sound was gone and she blinked rapidly to clear her head of the pain the startling noise caused.

The mech suit's face was a rough approximation of a human's face. It had circular eyes and a crescent mouth. No nose, although there was a small bulge where the nose should've been. Proportionally it was too tiny to be comforting. It really just looked like someone had punched from standing inside the suit's skull. The mech suit seemed to have a helmet around their head, although it was connected, and this gave the illusion that organic flowing hair might be held underneath. Which further fooled Harding's mind into seeing this thing as a humanoid instead of a bunch of boxes clotted together.

But the thing that really convinced Harding that this thing was, at a minimum, imitating a human was when its round eyes opened and neon purple light shined out of them.

The purple eyes looked over each of the three thetas. The groan started again but stopped before Harding's hands reached her ears. It came back quieter then got deeper before fading to silence. It returned and ascended a few octaves before getting so high that the shrill sound felt like a drill in the side of Harding's skull. It went silent in the cavernous containership.

Its purple eyes stared, unblinking, at the three people floating in front of it, as if it hadn't just sounded like a guitarist testing their amp and pushing it to its limits.

"Let's go," Thal said before kicking off the metal crates to make toward the gap in the crates they'd entered through. They waited for the other two to join them.

"What do you think it is?" Kunle asked. He kicked off the crates, but unlike Thal, he floated up to the suit's face.

Realizing how small Kunle was compared to just the machine's head made the suit sound like something that might wrap around a person. This suit at best might have a small cockpit, but since theta ships didn't transport living things this seemed unlikely. Then again if the suit had its own life support then a person could live inside this without needing redundant life support systems in the cargo container.

No. The purple, yellow, and red paint job meant this wasn't fleet equipment. At least not Alfavito Fleet equipment. And it was too big and advanced to be made by a private citizen or company. Anything with technology this advanced would be on a crowded planet that couldn't house a project this big. Any outpost with the space wouldn't have the tech. And anything built-in space would have the oversight of the fleet, making anything as exciting as purple a nonstarter.

This thing was alien, there was no doubt in Harding's mind about it.

Which meant it would be dangerous.

Which meant Thal was right.

The machine spouted some gibberish at the tiny thetas in front of it. Then said, "I come in peace," before spouting more gibberish.

"You come in peace," Harding said. Unwilling to make the same statement for her or her species.

"I am Eldron of the galfers," the machine said. "I've floated the void of space searching for intelligent life. What do you call yourselves? What is your species?"

"We can't tell it that," Thal said from the exit gap. "This thing should be talking to someone way above our pay grade."

To Harding, it felt like Thal was sticking around less out of curiosity and more like a babysitter or a spy preparing to tattle on her at the first opportunity. But you did what you could with the crew mates you were assigned.

"Come on Kunle," Harding said. "Let's get back to the LAM. Maybe the local archives will have some information on it." Harding kicked off towards Thal.

Kunle kicked off the mech suit and darted around from each limb superficially inspecting it. He looked like a gnat buzzing around a stoic farmer. The purple eyes followed him when they weren't looking at the thetas that had one foot out the door. Kunle eventually contented himself and darted off to his crew mates eventually leading them through the crates' passages back to the spine.

Floating back in silence Harding had time to think. She had no doubt that the local archives were empty on this matter. She didn't expect the cargo container's manifest to say much more.

And she didn't count on delivering the suit to give her any answers either.

***

Theta Harding stood on top of the spine of the delivery ship. The exterior was painted a brilliant white that stood out on the void black background of space around it. Theta Frangos and Theta Osmund were at the rear of the ship interacting with the engines through the simulation and steering the ship towards the buoy. Kunle and Ergo were standing on the spine with Harding ready to help if anything went awry.

Small streams of white were a few centimeters above her face. They moved like waves on the ocean making soft electrical buzzing sounds with each fluctuation in their path. The white streams represented the ship's shield, however, the actual shield wasn't visible to the naked eye.

The solar system of planets that sat just past the nose of the ship, and the cloud of dwarf exoplanets behind the ship also shouldn't have been visible to the naked eye. But that was the beauty of the LAM's navigation simulation. She didn't have to stand on the exterior of the ship to use its guns, she didn't have to wear a bulky space suit. She hardly had to put herself in harm's way. She was still safely strapped into the round table's chair behind the shield and the double hulls of the ship each of them made of three centimeter thick titanium. The ship would be dead in the sky before her body was threatened.

The ship was headed towards the buoy which orbited one of the rocky planets in this solar system. It would hold directions to the gamma ship that would be receiving the delivery, mech suit and all. Buoys like this were littered all over the galaxy. They held special subspace transmitters and receivers that couldn't be held on the ships themselves as travel through subspace would damage the sensitive transmitters.

Thal was at the head of the ship, closest to the buoy, prepared to receive their next directions. Their shouts, which sounded like Thal was right next to her, were too concerned to be related to the buoy's instructions.

"Three vassir battleships are incoming," Thal said.

As if Theta Thal's warning were an invitation three sharp-nosed alien battleships appeared out of thin air and loomed above the delivery ship. The ships were a sooty gray and looked like the barbed end of an arrow that was prepared to skewer the little delivery ship.

They were close and Harding wasn't surprised to find out this was not an enlarged view of the enemy ships like the planets were.

Harding rushed for a gun while Theta Frangos called out the maneuver he was about to pull with the ship's engine. Despite him being across the ship he spoke like he was right next to Harding, and every other theta.

"I'm using the buoy to transmit a distress signal," Thal said.

The enemy fire came like a lightshow of neon red lights. A flashing barrage of plasma light traveled in bolts of light nearly instantly across the space between the ships. The white streams of the shield above Harding flashed red every time one of the enemy's bolts struck it.

Harding returned fire with the turret she'd manned. Kunle and the other thetas that weren't transmitting or steering did the same.

But it was hopeless. They were one small delivery ship against three battleships. Battleships manned by the determined and proud vassirs; aliens that needed the same oxygen-rich earth-like planets that humanity liked to claim as their own.

The white streams of the shield were constantly red. Then the shields disappeared completely. That didn't stop the attack. The projected plasma bolts landed on the white surface of the theta ship. It left black scorch marks on the surface but that wasn't anything that wouldn't buff out.

The problem was when Harding started losing the view of the ship's exterior. Gaps in her vision started to appear like black boxes, spots where the LAM was blind to what was happening outside the silver cockpit.

The enemy fire was damaging the cameras and sensors. The plasma wouldn't bust through the titanium hull, and certainly wouldn't bust through both. But the attack was trying to blind the LAM, and its pilots, to the world outside.

A red bolt of plasma came straight for Theta Harding. She screamed and returned fire with her own bolts of plasma. It did nothing. The gun stopped firing. Her view of the outside world went black.

She stood inside the silver cockpit. She wasn't floating and there were no round table chairs. Only a bar-height round table that Thal, Frangos, and the others leaned on. The old-style cockpit was ornamental. A way for the crew to communicate with each other while still wired up to the LAM.

"What in the void do they want with our preserves?" Frangos asked. His frame was a little more filled out in the LAM, but he was still stick-thin and lanky. "They're not even going to be able to digest it."

"It's not the food they're after," Harding said. "They want the mech suit. Or whatever that groaning thing we found is."

"Why are we transporting a vassir target without a dozen Zeta battleships escorting us?" Frangos asked.

"I suppose that can go on the list of questions we'll never get the answer to," Harding said. "Is there anything on the exterior we can use to keep them off until some form of backup arrives?"

Frangos looked down at the table but whatever he saw wasn't being displayed to Harding. "Everything exterior is down. But I've got full control of our interior sensors. Pressure of the cargo container is wavering."

"Are they trying to cut into it?" Thal asked.

A video feed from inside the cargo container appeared in the air above the table. It appeared perpendicular to Harding's eye-line but she knew it was perpendicular to the other theta's eye-line as well since they looked up in the same direction.

The exterior wall of the container had a pill-shaped hole cut into it. Vassirs in maroon red space suits floated in using small jetpacks to navigate the large container. They looked humanoid with the exception of a spare arm coming off their back like a tail.

"They're using their remora ships to cling to the exterior of the container. It lets them create a seal so that the container isn't exposed to vacuum."

"Bummer," Harding said. "If it got exposed to vacuum the whole place would become a winter wonderland."

"Could we break the seal of the container and expose it to vacuum?" Thal asked.

Harding liked where their head was at. But Frangos was less enthusiastic. "The pressure to open the container is far more than the motors can bear. It doesn't have any venting systems like our ship because it's not supposed to be opened to the vacuum of space."

"We can't let them get away with this technology. The suit is sentient. It tried to communicate with us."

"So it's our prisoner and we don't want our enemy running away with it?" Frangos asked. "We don't even know if it will survive the vacuum of space."

"It can," Harding said, remembering the machine's comment about floating the void of space. "It's trying to make contact with something intelligent. And wouldn't we rather that intelligent thing be us over the vassir?"

"I'm sure the vassir would say the same about us," Frangos said.

"If we connect our container with the spine by opening the two hatches between the rooms we could then vent our spine to vacuum and the cargo container would be in vacuum as well." Harding had the inklings of a plan but didn't know how much good it would do her.

"No no no it's not that simple," Frangos said. "The vents that can expose the spine to vacuum aren't prepared to release that much air that fast. It'd blow every fist-sized vent into the size of a hatch"

"How big of a hole would we need?" Harding asked.

"This is ridiculous," Frangos said. "We'd have to jettison the engine and the cockpit."

"But you can do it?" Harding asked him.

"Sure, everything's modular. If something is overheating in the engine room we can jettison it and live on the float until a fleet of kappas come to repair us. The cockpit is effectively an escape pod, in case there's something wrong with the cargo or the engine's jettison. But even if we do both it won't work."

"Why not?"

"The spine's hatch isn't electronic. Someone would have to go and open it manually."

"Easy enough," Harding said.

***

And it should've been easy enough. Even with Theta Harding taking the time to put on a bulky space suit—at Theta Frangos' insistence. She pushed hard against the pipe she was using as a wrench to open the final dog clip. But it didn't budge from its locked position perpendicular to the rim of the hatch.

The orange and red hammocks floated in the weightless air of the spine and she wished she could be that carefree right now. She wished she could be snacking on some chili or even the preserves below that she was about to ruin. But right now Harding could only smell the sterile air of her suit's oxygen tank mixed with the nervous sweat she was throwing off in tiny spherical beads. The fabric of the suit crinkled with every move she made to push the final dog open.

Her vision was limited by the sides of the helmet. But it was an actual helmet this time not just a headrest that was nicknamed a helmet. Her heart raced as she could hear groaning and hissing and the clanging of remora ships clinging to the side of the cargo container. This was what she'd imagined she'd be doing when she joined the Alfavito Fleet against her father's wishes.

This was real. Real dangerous. But real.

Unfortunately, she was really running out of time. And Kunle, ever vigilant, had tightened down this last dog as hard as he could. She kicked against the tight walls of the spine. She clung to the ladder rungs and pulled herself against the pipe and the rung to get some leverage.

"Harding, you need to hurry up," Frangos said through the tiny speakers of the helmet. He was still in the LAM safe in the cockpit on the other side of the sealed hatch. "They've connected a remora large enough to extract the suit. Their doorway is almost completed."

With a few grunts and curses, Harding pulled against the wrench.

Harding slipped and banged her helmet against the ladder rung she was holding on to it echoed a thud around the room and her helmet.

She reached back for the wrench, her view of it obscured by the walls of the big helmet. When the pipe wasn't where she expected she took a closer look. The dog had slipped loose.

Immediately she pushed the lever the rest of the way and the hatch swung open up into the spine room.

"I'm in, open the cargo container hatch," she said to Frangos.

"Done."

The container hatch opened downward like a trap door. Harding immediately saw a half dozen maroon vassirs floating among the cargo containers.

"Vent it now," she said. She wanted them incapacitated before they saw that there was a quick and easy passage between the breached container and the crew's ship.

"Get back to the cockpit," Frangos said.

"No time. Vent it."

"No," Frangos said. "It'll suck you clear out into the void. We'll never find you in time."

Quite frankly Harding didn't care. Or she did care but a whole lot less than she cared about the crew getting captured because of her ambitious and hastily concocted rebellion.

"I'll hold on."

Frangos laughed at that. "You'd have to be strapped into something set up to hold a few kilonewtons of force."

"Sounds good," Harding said. The tropical orange hammocks fluttered in front of her face. She climbed into the closest one and strapped herself in. It was tough and she had to let out some slack on the straps to get it around the ankles of her suit's boots but she was secure enough after only a few seconds.

"Vent it," Harding repeated. She was floating lackadaisically in the hammock gripping onto it with her gloved hands as tight as she could.

"Alpha bless you," Frangos said.

Harding listened for the hiss of the airlock. It came and was instantly followed by the torrential roar of air rushing past her and her hammock. She billowed in the hurricane-force winds as every molecule of air rushed past her out of the front that once held the cockpit and the rear which once held the engine.

She flopped around. The rush of air pushed her spine against the direction it wanted to go. The gusts threw her arms every which way, her grip was helpless compared to the force of the air.

She was experiencing something real. Something more complicated and hectic than anything the LAM could simulate. A countless number of molecules rushed past her interacting with the fabric of her suit and her hammocks in ways that even the fastest computer couldn't predict. Air rushing past her helmet created sound waves through her suit that were noisy, chaotic, and unique to this instant of time.

Then it was over. It was silent. Harding was still.

White flecks of frost lazily floated around her inside the narrow corridor of the spine. The spine itself was merely a square pipe. Both ends were exposed. Her view was blocked by hammocks in the direction of the cockpit. But from the end which was formerly an engine room, she saw frosty white detritus that was once boxes and jars of preserves floating in the air around her.

The tiny speakers of her helmet crackled to life. "Theta ship 682, this is Gamma 817. We're engaging the enemy and sending a kappa ship to rescue your jettisoned cockpit."

"Should probably send someone to pick me up from the spine," Theta Harding replied.

And they did. The vassir didn't stay long after the Gamma ship arrived with a half dozen lower-ranking battleships in tow. They'd rushed to the theta's position through subspace.

Theta Harding was ordered to report to Gamma Parker after the medical team cleared her. She was physically fine and was now standing in the office of Gamma Parker.

Her heart raced with nerves but it was nothing compared to the rush she'd just experienced in the spine. The room smelled like cinnamon, a scent that Gamma Parker had seemed to infuse into every cubic centimeter of the room. It reminded Harding of her grandmother's Snickerdoodle cookies.

Gamma Parker was intimidating. His gray hair was combed neatly to the side, his face seemed to be covered in wrinkles frozen in a perpetual scowl. His dark green uniform was crisp and pressed as if any wrinkle would flee after a stern glance from the gamma.

The room itself was oval and styled after an office of similar shape. There was a lot of wooden furniture and a few cream-white couches. Gamma Parker sat behind his large wooden desk scowling at some paperwork.

Getting this much wood, let alone paper, would be prohibitively expensive, even for a Gamma like Parker. But that was the beauty of the LAM. It didn't have to be real to be experienced.

"Sir," Harding said since the man hadn't noticed her virtual appearance in his office.

"Are you aware of the damage you've caused?" Gamma Parker asked.

"Yes sir," Harding replied.

The oval office disappeared and the pair stood in the mist of white snowflakes. Six walls floated at a distance. They were not connected at the edges, instead, gaps of stars, or the gamma ship, could be spotted between the walls.

She was standing inside the cargo container. It'd been completely destroyed.

A few maroon vassir floated around stunned or worse. Kappas flew around energetically with their jetpacks thrusting them where they needed to go. They were collecting debris, vassir bodies, and disengaging the few crates that were still stuck to the floating walls.

Gamma Parker turned his gaze to look behind Theta Harding. She turned easily enough since she was standing instead of floating. Whatever camera was recording and projecting the work outside was high quality. Nearly every bit of floating pickled vegetable or shriveled-up preserved fruit was visible in her line of sight.

"Half the Alfavito is going to have to settle for freeze-dried preserves instead of the fresh stuff you were delivering."

"Sorry sir," Harding said.

The gamma took a few steps toward the cloud of freeze-dried preserves. Harding followed and found her stride was covering hundreds of meters of space. She stood in front of the giant purple and yellow mech suit.

"But then there's this," Gamma Parker said. "The vassir likely would've made off with it if you hadn't detonated a few tons of food in their faces."

"Thank you, sir. Is it important?" Harding asked.

"Of course it's important. Everything thetas deliver is important."

Harding watched a dozen kappas jetting around the thing. They were connecting straps to it so that they could tow it into the gamma ship's yawning dock.

"Can I know what that thing is?"

"No one knows what that thing is," Gamma Parker said. "And now that we know it's important to the vassir it will be so classified and well-guarded that no one in your generation will hear about it."

Harding looked at the large humanoid robot. It had a rime of frost on the sharp edges of its arms and chin. That added to the chaos of the colorful decals of flames and circuit boards and alien scripts that she'd never decipher or understand.

"You okay with not knowing, theta?"

"I know it's real. I know it's important," Harding said to her commander. "That's enough for me."

Keeping Life Alive

G erald McKinnly stood behind the hand-carved podium to call the meeting of the bunker families to order. The disaster happened five days ago; this was the first time everyone was in the same room. It was surprisingly tricky to get everyone together despite them all being confined underground.

The small group of fifty people had survived the nuclear disaster thanks to McKinnly's preparations. But in less than a week, fights had already broken out. No physical altercations yet, McKinnly and the handgun on his belt guaranteed none of that would be tolerated, but disagreements on who got which resources when had started. This meeting would address those problems.

"As potentially the only surviving members of humanity, it is imperative that we continue to get along and manage our resources wisely," the group, composed of his closest friends and their families, quieted down as he spoke. "I never wanted this bunker to be used, but us and the future generations of humanity that are to come thanks to our foresight will be—"

A crackle echoed through the small chamber room of the bunker as lights flashed. McKinnly rushed towards the fuse box on the wall to see what had failed so soon. He'd invested so much in this project he couldn't foresee anything failing this early on.

The crowd gasped. None of the fuses had blown, and the lights stayed on.

He turned to the podium and saw two floating figures standing behind it. They shimmered a dazzling purple and red and seemed to have specks of stars floating in them.

A high-pitched whine filled the room. McKinnly drew his gun while the rest of the crowd covered their ears. The noise became so deep that it shook his chest like those damn Escalades that used to roll down the streets playing music. He was glad those were no longer in existence, even if the roads were gone too.

"This seems to be an acceptable auditory range," one of the glowing figures said.

McKinnly wanted to take down whatever floated in front of *his* podium, but the pair being a cloud of gas, he didn't know what to aim at.

The two shapes transmuted their form into something that appeared humanoid but still had a reddish-purple hue to the skin. Instead of wisps of gas extending from their body, the creatures had a half dozen corporeal arms that seemed to come out of their back and everywhere.

"We come in peace, don't shoot, all that nonsense."

McKinnly shot anyway now that he had somewhere to aim.

The bullet stopped mid-air, and the resulting gunshot was muffled.

"I'm Grumbo, and this is Henley. We've come to clean up your planet," the being used its arms to gesture to itself and its companion.

"Clean it up?" McKinnly asked. "It's a nuclear wasteland."

"That's exactly how we were able to find you." the one called Henley replied. "The nuclear explosions that covered your planet were enough to notice you in the expansive void of space."

"We're contacted by alien life less than a week after we blew ourselves out of existence," someone in the audience said.

"You couldn't have come a few months earlier?" McKinnly asked. "Knowing other life was in the universe would have changed everything."

"A few months ago, you were just a cold rock floating in space."

"But we had cities, satellites, and radio waves," McKinnly protested.

Grumbo made something that looked like a shrug, "lots of planets have those."

"Anyway, we've cleaned your planet up," Henley sounded proud. "We've got a few more to do this afternoon."

"You can't just clean up a planet full of nuclear waste," McKinnly dismissed.

"They did," Johnson's kid said. He was in charge of monitoring the few sensors they had on the planet's surface. "It's still a mess out there, but the radiation and dust in the atmosphere all settled down. Everything keeping us down here is fixed."

"It should just look like a comet hit the planet a few dozen years ago," Grumbo explained.

"Why did you choose to reveal yourselves to us in this bunker?" McKinnly asked. Surely his preparedness had earned him an audience with these beings, or maybe they were the only ones left. He hoped they'd forgive him for his earlier transgression.

"We appeared to all the civilizations on this planet we could find. All in all, there's maybe 14 million of you left," Henly answered.

"Not too bad, the last planet we left had only a half dozen survivors," Grumbo added.

"Although they were a hive-like being with trillions of worker drones."

"You'd think they'd be able to get along considering the whole hive–"

"Wait, there's other intelligent life out there besides you and us?" McKinnly asked.

"Of course! Did you really think you were the only ones in the entire universe?"

"And they're all blowing themselves up with nukes?" Johnson's kid asked.

"A surprising number of them do that," Henly replied.

"Keeps us pretty busy," Grumbo added. "We show up and clean up. Keeping sentient life alive is surprisingly difficult."

"Why don't you warn them?" McKinnly was unimpressed by these beings' approach to their task. "You should tell them that there are others?"

"We tried that. Then they just used the nukes on us," Henley said. "Say, didn't we already come to this planet?"

"Maybe a few million years ago. The habitants were a little bigger back then," Grumbo replied.

"Are you talking about dinosaurs?" Johnson's kid asked.

"It couldn't be the dinosaurs," McKinnly said. "A comet knocked them out."

Grumbo disgustingly distorted his face then it landed on a smile-like shape. "Try to do better than them this time around."

Boulders in the Stream

Talamade sat on the well-padded banquet chair as waitstaff brought out plates of jolfé. The room was buzzing with conversation after the last speaker's announcement about two new schools opening on Elani.

Talamade's table was far from the stage and mostly empty. The university had offered complimentary tickets to this banquet. He took up the offer hoping to meet with conglomerate project managers. Specifically project managers that could get him assigned to other geological survey projects like the one he'd successfully completed on Elani. He had no desire to go back to Elani, as it was currently the most undeveloped planet in the Central System.

He recognized a few other faces in the room and the mostly empty table indicated the university's tickets were not in demand. Two women sat across the table from him laughing about some shared experience they'd had while on Elani. Their stories sounded like they were teachers at the planet's capital city, the most common job on the planet for off worlders. The Central System established positions teaching pre-university courses but also skilled labor and even advanced research positions were being filled. All to prepare for the wildcat colony's first population infusion.

The only other person at the half full table sat next to him. Her elbow rubbed his with every bite she took. She was tall with wide shoulders like most Elanies. Talamade had felt dwarfed by almost everyone that came from the planet despite his average stature. She'd introduced herself as Gabriella when she first sat down but they hadn't had much time to get to know each other due to the parade of speakers across the stage.

Neither of them were engaged in the teacher's conversation. They used slang and constantly skipped the climactic parts of their stories, focusing on reacting to the ridiculousness more than recounting the events. It was clear they were catching up, not trying to share stories with the table.

"Tastes like week old porridge," Gabriella said after taking a bite out of the jolfé. Her speech was accented but hadn't diverged from Common Tongue so much that it was incomprehensible. Her comment didn't interrupt the teachers but it caught Talamade by surprise.

He spooned some into the bakan leaf. He'd never gotten the hang of scooping the rice up with just the leaf, even though Elanies made it look effortless. He took a bite. The bakan leaf wasn't nearly as bitter as what grew on Elani, and the rice was sweeter without the sharp pricks of spicy peppers. "It's not so bad," Talamade admitted.

Gabriella buzzed her lips, launching spittle out. Talamade ignored her gesture and hoped nothing had landed on his plate; for the first time he might actually finish all of this jolfé. The pair across the table stopped their conversation and laughed like they were watching a comedy from the net.

"If you were teaching in the capital schools then surely you had jolfé at Hibbera's," Gabriella said. "It's the only place worth eating near the CS schools."

"I'm actually a geologist," Talamade clarified. The teachers went back to their conversation excitedly talking about a mischievous student well known at their school, uninterested in a geologist's experience on Elani. "I was on the bay side of the city when I was there." He'd also spent most of his time eating ration bars to avoid the local flavors.

"The fish is very good in that part of town," she said. "Did you try any antui?"

Antui was a dish he'd heard about before he ever shipped off on the assignment. Elani's fish were misshapen and had scrawny bodies with large heads that were considered divine. Locals skewered the fish and roasted them with tangy seasonings. The Elanies ate the snacks at least twice daily; he didn't have the guts to look something in the eyes while he ate it.

"Unfortunately, I didn't get the chance to try any."

"You'd have to go out of your way to avoid eating it. I hope your teachers can give our youngest generation that sort of dedication."

Gabriella chuckled to herself as she folded a leaf around some more of the jolfé. "What did you like about Elani? Or was it just the paycheck that brought you there."

"No, no, it wasn't that. I thought the whole place was beautiful. I haven't seen a planet so peaceful from orbit. And I've never gotten to fly over such dense forests."

"Peaceful?" Gabriella started snacking on the large bits of palmu roots in the jolfé. "When I came here the whole dark side was lit up brighter than the stars in the void. Our planet likely looks quite dim from your perspective, with only one city shining into the dark."

"Most colonies appear that way before their fourth or fifth population infusion," Talamade said.

"That takes what? Forty or Fifty years?" Gabriella's words were fast and accented. A little calmer she said, "Elani was established generations ago, independently."

Talamade, and every other Central System citizen, was surprised they'd lasted that long. Elani's first settlers left before the Central System was established, when space travel was new and only a few conglomerates funded it.

Wildcat colonies, rogue ships that independently settled a planet and silently established a colony without communication or interaction with the Central System, were rare and dangerous. When wildcats were caught now they were charged for contract defection or misallocation of life. However, Elani's original conglomerate had gone bankrupt in the first Industrial War so Elani was invited into the Central System independent of all other conglomerates.

"And it's quite impressive that you've survived so long alone in the void." He immediately regretted the words. They'd seemed like a compliment in his head but sounded dismissive as he spoke them aloud.

Gabriella made the dismissive spittle again. "How could we not? " She pushed some of the food around on her plate as if she was searching for a taste of home in the dish. "It's not a planet terraformed to be Earth-like. It's naturally Earth-like making it rare since it has plants we can digest, fish we can eat, and a comfortable climate."

Comfortable was not how Talamade would describe the climate, nor the shacks that he had to sleep in while there. "Elani is quite beautiful. A guide took me up a mountain road one day and I could look across the whole valley that the capital sat in."

"Was it Beckdale's pass or Hitomi ridge?" Gabriella asked. There was an excitement in her eyes brighter than a kid's on Elder's Day.

"I'm not sure," Talamade answered after trying to remember what the guide told him months ago. "But I could see all the intertwining roads, patches of neighborhoods, the capitol building and the elevator being constructed near it. It was all sitting in a sea of green bakan trees and palmu vines." He was sure there were other plants and trees there too but couldn't remember their names either.

"That damn elevator takes up half the view from the ridge," she waved her long arms like she was going to tear it down herself. Getting another chortle out of the teachers. "You must have gone to the pass. They should have built it outside the city or not at all. Don't see what the problem with the current launch pad is."

"Launch pads are slow and use up too much fuel. Once the space elevator is built, getting things in and out of orbit will be a breeze." There was no way Gabriella didn't already know that though.

"It's just another technology they're forcing onto us. Like the schools and the hand terminals." She grabbed her terminal out of her pocket and tossed it on the table as if it was a piece of dirty dish going in the recycler. "All for what purpose? So we can travel to places like this? To sit in small chairs and eat bland jolfé?"

"It's not like the Central System forced itself onto Elani," Talamade said. "Your leadership agreed to let the elevator be built."

The Central System held reverence towards all sapient life since it was so rare in the cosmos. The Central System did everything in its power to eliminate war, famine, and disease so that humanity could prosper. Earth-like planets were rare, and not every planet in a goldilocks zone could be terraformed. Despite this it was made clear early on and often that the wildcat colony on Elani would not be forced into the Central System or any existing conglomerate despite the countless humans the planet could sustain.

"The councilors that agreed to it weren't working with Elani's best interest at heart," Gabriella replied. "Most of them now live here or somewhere else in the Central System. It's unlikely they'll ever step on Elani soil again. But at least they can't get a good meal."

"You can't know everything that they had to take into consideration. I'd never assume I could make the tough decisions minister judges have to make with every trial."

"No, I don't think you could." Gabriella let out a friendly chuckle. "But I know that within a year of the Central System finding us half of the eldest council was replaced by new members. Members that had met with CS ambassadors and ministers."

"Younger generations always embrace change easier and you can't adopt a technology you don't understand." Many of his senior professors had a hard time adopting the newest research equipment.

"You sound like the first speaker of this evening." Gabriella's tone indicated it wasn't a compliment. "Maybe they were acting in our best interest. But a bakan tree doesn't grow large leaves by leaving room for other plants."

"Then why don't you become a councillor and change things?" Talamade wasn't sure if Elani usually had women politicians but the

Central System would have implemented equity laws as a prerequisite to giving them new technology.

"I plan to, like my grandmother before me, but spices mixed into the pot can't be taken out."

"But if everyone on the planet feels the way you do then you can take action to separate yourself from the Central System," Talamade said.

There were a few self-sufficient conglomerates that operated independently of the Central System. They were able to provide universal basic quantities of food, water, medicine, living space, and data communication access to all its citizens. By providing all basic needs the Central System had no reason to be involved. The Farook conglomerate had been doing it for a dozen generations.

"Unfortunately, I think once everyone sees your technology, medicine, and climate controlled buildings they'll want it for themselves just like our leaders did." Her wide shoulders slumped.

"And what's so bad about that? You don't want your people to know their great grandparents?" Talamade asked. With life extension drugs where they were today he had photos of his great great grandparents holding him as a child, even though he never knew them.

"Don't question my love for my people." Her tone was sharp. "The cost of these luxuries is too high."

"The System is sending it to you for free."

"The cost is infusions of people like you who come and only see bakan trees and valleys. But unlike you they don't leave when the job is done." She moved her hands under the table.

To Talamade it looked unnatural for an Elani to say something passionate without a large gesture.

"Do you know what I see when I hike Beckdale's pass?" She finally asked.

"No," Talamade said timidly. He couldn't imagine it was any different from his view even if she'd hiked it before Central System EVs were introduced.

"I saw a neighborhood of homes I helped build with my sisters for our neighbors on their wedding days. I could point to shops where boys bought me antui and palmu flowers before harvest festivals. I could watch the flow of fishermen bringing their catches to market trading for bags of rice from the paddies or salves for their loved ones."

"The Central System isn't taking that away. Your memories of these places and Elani's traditions will remain."

Gabriella buzzed her lips in frustration. "It's not the memories I cherish, it's the interactions between the people. Already house printers are being built in torn down neighborhoods. Teenagers are buying gems and metals to court each other, antui is sold for intangible credits stored on computers, and it's difficult to have a harvest festival when foreign food is grown year round in vats." Gabriella let out a sigh. "I'm not technophobic. My grandmother was a midwife who continued to look for ways to reduce infant and mother mortality. I saw the change her innovations brought. I know your medicine and terminals will change our lives.

"I just wish you didn't say it was free. Because the price is hordes of people who only see the bakan trees and the rocks in the ground. I don't want you to love our food or speak our language. Every time a foreigner winces at the bitterness of bakan leaves my heart smiles."

Talamade had no doubts about her sincerity. Her entire body, from her eyebrows to her broad shoulders, seemed to beam with that statement. "So if you wind up in power you'll balance those two things?" he asked.

"I'll try, but Elani is only half the equation. The Central System needs to see Elanies too, not just our medical and technical needs but our interactions and culture. My biggest fear is that you were right when you said my leaders were acting with our best interest at heart. I'm here to figure that out. I'd rather be spending time with my nieces and nephews but I want to make sure they have a chance to know about the beautiful world their great grandmother took part in."

The stage's microphone buzzed as another speaker began discussing how delicious the meal was. After a few more speeches, cocktails were served while people mixed together chatting about one thing or another. Talamade made small conversations here or there with project managers from the research company he'd worked for. But the whole time his eyes drifted among the crowd watching Gabriella and other Elanies' hulking forms stick out above the crowd like rocks in a stream. He hoped that she didn't get worn down by the flow of the water. She didn't seem like the kind of person who could be worn down. He hoped that like a boulder that fell into a stream, she'd change the course of the river.

Gabriella's words echoed in his mind as a starship manufacturer asked: "Are the metals in their soil high enough quality that it'd be worth setting up a manufacturing satellite?"

"Elani is an absolutely remarkable place," Talamade said, "but it will cost far more than it's worth to get an operation set up there."

Unlike the water droplets in a river, he could work to make room for the boulder.

Debris Sea

A rare glimmer of sun snuck in from the thick glass panes of the council room's window.

Rare was a day when the kingdom of Sithab got more than an hour of sunlight. The kingdom was constantly under the looming threat of clouds prepared to rain, actively raining, or just finished raining.

And on the rare occasions that the clouds dispersed, the thick field of ancient metal debris blocked any attempt that the sun made to get through to the citizens of the kingdom.

Leading to rare glimmers of sunlight and hope that found their way to the surface.

Dannika Laskan, Sithab's master wizard, only master wizard, found a way to make the most of those small glimmers of hope. But lately, even her best efforts drew her hope tight as a mandolin string and thin as a cobweb.

But, strained as it was, it was still there. Especially today.

The pilot had survived today's launch. The ship hadn't, but the pilot had. And that meant she'd made a bit of progress. And as her former master had said: "Much like the debris field a lot of small progress can build into something remarkable."

Unfortunately, King Ramsey and General Klader didn't see it that way.

Which was why the king was slamming his fist on the thick wooden table to emphasize his point. The thick wooden armchair he sat in didn't shake under his shouts and frustrations, but about everything else in the room did, including the king's jowls and his attendant.

Unfortunately, the other thing that stood still in the room was General Klader. He sat across the table from her next to the king wearing the white and gold silk robes of his station he smiled like a barn cat who'd cornered a mouse.

The only thing creepier than Klader's smile was his hooked-nosed advisor Galeb who stood behind him, against the wall, listening, and most likely, scheming to see how he may turn the tide of this conversation to his and his general's favor.

Dannika did her best to stay still as the king shouted. She shouldn't act like a young maiden easily startled. She was a gray-haired master wizard, one of the most clever women in the whole country. Anywhere else she'd be a spinster with a dozen cats. If only she trusted the little beasts. If only she left a good puzzle alone.

But her age and wisdom didn't make the king's shouting any less uncomfortable.

Adding to that discomfort was her wooden chair and her wet woolen robes. The robes were soaked from the rain at the launch and were beginning to itch. If she didn't get them dry by a fire soon they'd begin to mildew.

But the smell wouldn't stand out in Sithab. This room smelled, like most rooms in the kingdom, of earthy mildew and moss. The lichens had found their way into every corner and crack of the castle's large stone walls. It'd take powerful magic or an unfathomable string of bone-dry days to even consider driving it out.

The king's pounding and shouting echoed through the cavernous council room. Dannika couldn't blame him, she was frustrated as well, but he couldn't see the promise of today's launch.

"We are down to the last of our ships. How many more failures will you make me endure wizard?" King Ramsey asked.

"We should employ the ships and their material for military application," General Klader butted in. "Using them will guarantee a successful invasion of Bryn D'wall."

It was only the third time he'd made that pitch this afternoon. The king hadn't agreed the past two times. But that didn't stop the knight from throwing his hook back in the water.

To Dannika it was ridiculous to believe that the neighboring kingdom of Bryn D'wall had any more riches than Sithab. This small continent hardly held enough space and resources for the two kingdoms. Which is why Renfro was so adamant and spent his life researching how to break through the sea of debris.

"Your Highness, there are more things we can try," Dannika pleaded. "If I can get these ships to work there will be far more valuable things in the heavens than in Bryn D'wall. There's no need to terrorize our neighbors and send young soldiers to their deaths."

"Need I remind you that the pillaging of Bryn D'wall is what covers the expenses of your experiments?" The king asked.

"And that you've killed just as many of my men with your failed launches than these invasions have," Klader added.

"Today's pilot survived," Dannika reminded them. He was covered in burns and had countless broken bones. But he was in the infirmary, alive, and breathing. "The launch next week will go better. I'm sure of it."

The general scoffed. "We're going to let these charades continue?... your majesty."

The king's brow was furrowed like a spring thunderhead about to drench the countryside. Dannika's chair creaked under her as she fidgeted nervously.

"I can learn from the pilot, sire," Dannika said, straining the little hope she had.

"You've had plenty of time to learn, charlatan. The debris is just too chaotic for you to navigate," Klader replied.

"The debris is proof that someone has pulled—"

King Ramsey silenced the wizard by lifting his hand. Faded blue robes hung loose from his arm.

"I will allow another attempt at the launch," the king said.

Dannika let out a sigh of relief.

"But," the king continued, "we will begin diverting resources towards the siege of Bryn D'wall."

"Your majesty, I need those—" Dannika started.

"Be glad that you have what you do," the king said. "I would've fired you ages ago if I hadn't promised Renfro that I'd put as much as this kingdom could spare into overcoming the debris."

Even from the grave, her old master was sheltering her from the worst of the downpour.

The king stood up indicating there'd be no further discussion or lobbying from either side of the table.

Dannika rushed to stand up and bow. Her robe caught on a chair and it clattered behind her in her haste.

The only response to that in the room was from Dannika, whose cheeks turned flush red in the embarrassment.

General Klader, graceful as ever, stood and bowed to the king, adding some groveling comments under his breath, no doubt at Dannika's expense.

2

Renfro's workshop was warm and dry thanks to the evening's fire, which had burned to dim but hot embers by now. Dannika still thought of it as her master's workshop even though she'd been the only tenant for five years now.

Her supper, a vegetable stew, simmered away over the hot coals. The room was filled with the scent of rich herbs and she could already taste the tender potatoes and carrots.

Small fireless lamps hung from the wooden rafters. They gave off no heat but made the room as bright as day and let her work late into the night. Which was necessary if she wanted to make any progress in next week's launch.

Her robes hung near the hearth, she now wore a thin summer cloak which was just thick enough to keep the worst of the night's chill out.

Pops of the embers interrupted the long creaks of the wooden turbine turning outside. The day's rain meant the stream next to the workshop ran strong this evening. Dannika was encouraged by the sound of the weary turbine. It meant that there'd be plenty of magic stored up tonight for her to use in preparation for the next launch.

The turbines were one of Renfro's greatest inventions. They generated a power that brought the kingdom's relics to life. Including the ship that Dannika was trying to get past the debris.

The king had countless treasures from holograms to magical swords that could slice through a man's armor. Renfro's inventions hadn't helped the common man like he'd hoped but he always thought that more treasures awaited in the heavens and reaching for them would help everyone from the farmers to the fighters.

Despite not achieving that goal he was remembered fondly by the king, the court, and everyone that knew him. Especially Dannika.

And she was worried she'd be remembered as the wizard who was beheaded if she didn't get the ship through the debris field soon.

Which is why she was eager to watch the recording of today's launch.

Dannika had done her best to clear the center of the room. Parchment, lifeless magical relics, and long snake-like cords had filled it when she arrived. Finding a home for everything was always a challenge despite the countless shelves that Renfro had installed.

But she needed to make as much space as possible so that she could watch the recording of the day's launch.

A perfectly smooth sphere the color of pipe smoke sat on a custom metal pedestal in the center of the room. A grid of buttons was inset into the side of the pedestal and Dannika could control the images projected into the room with them. The markings on them meant nothing to her, but she'd memorized their commands as a young apprentice.

She turned a switch near the magic storage devices. The lights in the rafters turned off. They would interfere with the crystal ball's projections. Plus pulling too much magic out of storage at once could cause fires.

She flipped another switch to direct magic to the crystal ball in the center of the room.

The room came to life with a mossy green light. A list of ancient phrases was projected onto the wall above the fireplace. Dannika scrolled through them to find the most recent one. The one from today's launch.

Once she selected the right ancient phrase the ship appeared between her and the dim fireplace. It was a miniature version of the real thing, the size of her forearm, whereas the real thing was the size of a small house.

The ship rested on a simulated grass field that covered the workshop's wooden floor like a ghostly rug. Dannika could see a small version of herself, the king, his court, and General Klader.

The ship itself was smooth and flat like a river stone. Dannika's working theory was that, like a river stone, it needed to let wind, which seemed similar to water, flow around it.

The ship didn't have wings like a bird. Instead of flapping anything to get off the ground glowing orbs from underneath it pushed it into the air where it could float like a honey bee until the pilot flew it into the sky.

A thumb-sized version of the pilot climbed up the wooden stars into the cockpit. A fine crystalline dome came over him so that he could see out of every side. It was most similar to glass but was significantly clearer and thinner than the best windows in the palace.

The pilot gave a thumbs up to show all the instruments, at least all the instruments they knew how to read, were reporting ideal figures. The pilot commanded the ship to come to life. Orbs at the bottom of the ship glowed to life lifting the ship a half inch off the workshop floor.

In real life, the ship would be just above Dannika's head. And in real life, the orbs would be ruby red, instead of the dark emerald that the green projection made them out to be in the workshop.

Patches of grass in the launch field shriveled and burnt from the heat of the lift-off despite the wet drizzle that'd droned on since morning.

Once the ship was stable miniature Dannika gave the miniature ship the signal to go.

The ship climbed in the sky and floated at Dannika's eye level as the grass rug disappeared from the projection's field of view. The ship entered the clouds, which were projected as ethereal green mist that surrounded Dannika. Then the clouds soon fell away leaving the ship floating in the center of the room.

This was where Dannika had lost sight of the ship this morning. But thanks to the recording, which existed on the crystal ball through some unfathomable magic, she could watch the pilot like a goddess.

Green debris rained down from the workshop's rafters.

At first, it was a few, like a summer afternoon storm. The pilot avoided the largest pieces, smaller pieces hit the ship but didn't seem to do much damage to the ship.

The debris became bigger and more frequent like a hail storm of ancient relics. The pilot was good, his reflexes were sharp. She'd seen countless other pilots get knocked out of the sky by this point.

He'd done something clever, only a few pilots had figured out how to do it. The glowing orbs that had once been at the bottom of the ship had migrated to the back. This let the pilot fly straight up exposing the smallest amount of his ship to the debris above him.

It likely also gave him the speed he needed to escape the pull of gravity that kept humankind locked to the earth. Gravity that for some unexplained reason, didn't seem to apply to this debris.

But the faster the pilot flew the harder it was for him to react to every piece of debris.

Dannika slowed the recording down so that it didn't look like a hare avoiding a hound. And even at the slowest setting, it was still tough for Dannika to keep up with what was going on. She'd be watching this many more times tonight.

The pilot shot at the debris with the guns that the general was so excited about. Every pilot attempted it, every pilot learned that it was futile. Large pieces broke apart and made more obstacles while small pieces seemed to hold together, too strong to be broken down further.

The debris was thick now, even in the slowed-down recording it was like a green fog had rolled into the workshop. The pilot's tiny head switched back and forth like a leaf in the wind.

He dodged a few large pieces, then a chunk of metal, maybe originally it was part of a larger ship, came at his right side where he wasn't looking.

Dannika saw the miniature version of the pilot jerk his head at the last second. He was slow to react. This was the piece that knocked him out of the sky.

At least that's what Dannika expected.

The ship jerked to the left and the debris missed the glass dome by a hair. Dannika watched it again, thinking it was a glitch in the recording but each time the ship did the same thing, she couldn't spot any other anomalies.

The pilot's hands, which she could see by zooming in very close to the cockpit, didn't seem to be doing anything. From the look on his face, he seemed as baffled as Dannika that he hadn't crashed.

But unfortunately, his luck ran dry.

The jerking motion had moved him into the path of another piece of large debris that cut into the bottom of the ship.

The ship smoked, the glowing orbs powered down, and the ship stuttered in the air before falling back to the ground. Green clouds rushed past as debris disappeared into the rafters.

Once through the clouds, the pilot ejected himself from the ship. Dannika had watched this part from the ground. She remembered the pilot floating down to earth with a large canvas sack over his head to catch the air.

Riders galloped away from the launch pad following the trajectory of the ship so that it could be recovered, or at the very least, didn't fall into the "wrong" hands.

Dannika moved back in time through the recording and watched the jerking motion again and again. By the time she'd remembered her dinner the fire all but died out and the stew was cold.

She didn't care though.

She'd just discovered something new the ship could do.

Now she needed to be the wizard Renfro trained her to be and understand it, control it, use it to get through the debris.

And she only had a week.

3

The legend of the voices in the mountains is told to every Sithab child when they inevitably ask about the king's powerful relics, the flying stone, and the mystical wizards that make it all work.

Generations ago a shepherd was leading his flock through the rocky Ragnar mountains that divided the kingdoms of Sithab and Bryn D'wall.

The shepherd, either too lazy to get the work done on time or rebelliously pushing his luck (depending on how the child hearing the story had acted that day), was caught in an afternoon thunderstorm high on the mountain.

With no way to get his flock down the mountainside quick enough he took shelter in one of the many caves of the Ragnar mountains. With most of his flock hemming and hawing about the storm he didn't notice the demonic voices and noises at first.

But once he heard them only the dangerous lightning outside kept him from fleeing the haunted cave.

Before the storm had completely receded he rushed out of the cave with as much of the flock that was willing to follow him. At this point, he was more concerned for his safety than the goats and sheep he herded. At best the ones left behind would be a sacrifice to the demons that let him shelter in the cave.

Once in the town, he found a dozen other shepherds and farmers to return and drive the demons away. Whether they were being brave or were just convinced the young shepherd was making up a reason to keep the best grazing fields of the mountain to himself, is unknown.

They followed him with heirloom swords and their sharpest scythes. Prepared for the worst, hoping for the best.

What they found was unlike anything they could've prepared or hoped for.

The farmers descended into the cave with their torches and lanterns throwing dim light into the winding caverns.

After an hour or so of climbing down a stair-like path, they found the source of the noise.

A cavern the size of a palace ballroom was filled with smooth ships the size of stables. They made demonic whirring noises and beeped incessantly. The ships spoke in ancient tongues that even today's wizards have yet to decipher.

The shepherds and farmers tried to destroy the ships, as most humans do when faced with things they don't understand. But the protective shells of the ships were too strong for even the largest swords and the strongest farmers.

The group returned to town shaken by what they saw and requested rare gunpowder and dynamite from their sovereign so that they may destroy the demons, or at least lock them away behind a wall of exploded rubble.

But when the king and his advisors got word of strange impenetrable beasts in the mountains of Ragnar they saw an opportunity to tame the beasts and gain an upper hand over Bryn D'wall.

The king demanded that the treasure be claimed for him and the kingdom of Sithab before Bryn D'wall shepherds found them. The king's archeologists and wizards removed the beasts and ancient relics from the cave. But have yet to tame the beasts in a way that serves the king's purposes.

Countless other treasures were uncovered deep within the Ragnar mountains. Treasures that wizards still toil over today.

And the citizens of Sithab, or at least its rulers, hope that one day a relic will be the key to conquering Bryn D'wall. They long for more land to conquer, and with the northern tundras and southern wasteland the only place to go is east to conquer Bryn D'wall.

Renfro, and now Dannika, merely hope that one of the relics might unlock a way to conquer the tundra, wasteland, or debris field above, so that the common citizen, whether they be of Sithab or Bryn D'wall, might know peace.

But as Dannika caught up to her master in age she found it less and less likely that the rulers would end their quest to conquer without a significant change in perspective.

And late at night when Dannika couldn't sleep she wondered how her master hadn't lost faith that peace was even an option.

4

Dannika stood behind a large pillar in the barrack's infirmary. It was once a building of the ancients, with its smooth stone floor, metal piping throughout, and massive windows of glass stained with color.

The large room was lined with beds, most of which were thankfully empty. A fire was burning in a large fireplace. The fireplace itself was added on with rough bricks held together with clay. How the ancients heated their living quarters without a fire was still a mystery.

The fire filled the heavy smooth stone walls with heat and the room was dry and comfortable despite the heavy storm pouring outside and rattling against the wooden shutters latched closed over the window.

Dannika wanted to speak to the pilot Yensha about his flight yesterday. She'd wanted to do it first thing this morning but guiding the repair of the ship for the upcoming launch had taken up her whole morning. Thankfully the storm got bad enough to stop progress and she was free to visit the pilot.

Despite Dannika's eagerness, she was now hesitant to leave the cover of the large pillar. General Kalder was speaking with the pilot, and his voice echoed confidently through the cavernous room.

"Were the guns powerful enough to take down stone walls?" Klader asked.

Whatever Klader was interested in it wouldn't be good for her.

"I think so, sir." the pilot replied.

"How was the navigation, could you avoid artillery fire?"

"The ship's shell is tough but somehow thinner than our armor. I hit debris the size of cannonballs without a problem, sir."

"If it's so strong how'd it get knocked out of the sky?" Klader asked.

The young pilot spoke timidly and it was difficult to hear him clearly from Dannika's hiding spot. "The piece that took me down was the size of a horse and moved twice as fast, sir. It was my mistake. I'm sorry to have damaged another one of your ships, sir."

"It's not your fault sonny," the general said with the superficial sincerity he used in the advisor meetings. "I am sure that the wizard's contraption had a flaw or two in it."

"Maybe, sir," the pilot said, reluctant to disagree with his leader's authority and willingness to cut him slack.

"If anyone asks that's the official story," the general said. "I'm doing my best to keep more soldiers like you from going up, being injured, or dying."

"It's a magnificent tool," the pilot said. "Flying it was like nothing else."

Dannika had heard enough. She stepped out from behind the column. The general's back was to the door and by the time he heard her coming, it looked like she'd entered from the arching doorway. No need for Klader to know she'd heard any of that.

The general grinned at her arrival and his wolfish smile would scare off even the bravest watchdog. His jaw was as sharp and square as an ancient brick, his robes were pure white and remarkably dry considering the storm outside.

Pilot Yensha looked worse today than he had when they pulled him out of the cockpit seat. She'd spent the whole morning guiding assistants in the repair of the ship, including reinstalling that seat. Still, she couldn't get what she'd seen in the crystal's recording off her mind.

She hoped the pilot would have an explanation for the jerking motion she saw on the recording.

The window above his bed was latched shut to keep the downpour that was raging outside at bay. Still, the wind rattled the wood in the window frame as if some specter was trying to enter.

The boy lay in a small hay bed under thick sheepskins. A small lamp hung on the wall behind him and cast just enough light to illuminate his black and blue face.

A white cloth covered the burns on his arm and neck. His leg was wrapped in a clay cast to keep the broken bones from moving and repairing incorrectly. It was elevated on some padding to help with swelling. Dannika hoped that was enough to get and keep the pilot on his feet.

Pilot Yensha probably would not have to fight in General Klader's invasion of Bryn D'wall. But Dannika doubted the young man considered this a favor.

"Will I get to fly again, sir?" the pilot asked hopefully.

"I'm sure you will, just not on a mission so risky."

"Of course," Dannika said, "he'll be using it to terrorize the citizens of Bryn D'wall."

"Only out of necessity and retaliation. This continent is too small to be divided, the king merely wants order to be restored."

Dannika wrinkled her nose like he was serving her month-old haggis.

"And the king's order can only be restored by brave young men like Yensha here. May the elders heal you soon," Klader said to the pilot.

"But this isn't something we'd expect a wizard to understand," Klader said to Dannika. "Your kind has always had heads so high in the sky you can't think straight with the debris beating against it," Klader said.

"I'd rather beat my head against problems than sink to bashing other's heads against rocks," Dannika said.

"Don't worry we'll be using something far more elegant than rocks very soon," the general said as his thick boots echoed through the infirmary.

"Sorry about him," the pilot said uncomfortable with the interaction.

"Sorry about your injuries. Are you okay?"

"They say I'll be fine, but might walk with a limp for a while."

"I'm sorry to hear that."

"I can still fly with a limp though," he said.

His eyes full of the wonder that most of the surviving pilots had. She hadn't gone up in a ship yet but she was still familiar with the excitement. It infected her every time she and Renfro discovered something new about the ancient relics.

"I wanted to ask you a question about the crash if you don't mind," she said.

"Of course, anything I can do to help."

"Before you crashed debris came from the right side."

The pilot nodded.

"You dodged it with a jerking motion. I've never seen a ship move like that. How'd you do it?"

"The angels were guiding the ship in that moment," the pilot responded with finality and reverence.

"Mhmm," Dannika said, hoping the pilot would add something to his explanation. The angels were a common explanation that pilots used to describe what miracles the ship performed. Dannika had enough experience with ancient relics that she knew it was just as likely to be demons, the wind, or just a pesky cat.

"The angel pushed you into another piece of debris," Dannika added when it was clear the pilot wasn't going to expand on his explanation.

"There wasn't an angel on that side to protect me," the pilot said.

The pilot stated the explanation with sincerity and Dannika had to hold herself back from laughing. She'd learned early on as a wizard not to dissect laypeople's logic, even when it seemed ridiculous. It was tough to enunciate the difference between the magic the wizards worked with and the miracles the people believed in.

"And how do you know there wasn't an angel on that side?" Dannika asked.

"You know, the lights around the cockpit," the pilot said.

Dannika did not know. She asked for clarification.

"There are small yellow lights surrounding the cockpit. They hold the angels' spirits. They were not lit up in the direction that the debris hit me."

Dannika was familiar with the lights he spoke of. But he'd attached some deeper meaning than was reasonable. They were just there to light up the cockpit, like most lights that ancient technology used.

At least that's what she'd always thought. But she'd never been in a ship pelted by debris. The pilot's logic was glitchy, but he had experience she didn't. And she wouldn't be a good wizard if she didn't take the clue he offered.

"If you could convince angels to protect that side of the ship they'd be able to protect us as we moved through the debris, no doubt," the pilot said.

Dannika nodded her head in agreement. It was always difficult to tell which parts of the ancient relics were operational and why.

"Thank you very much for your help and your service. May the Elders heal you soon," Dannika said as she turned to make her way to the exit.

"Wizard... when will the ship be repaired? Can I go back up soon?"

Dannika frowned, unwilling to face the injured man. "I think the ship will be repaired quicker than you."

The pilot's sigh seemed to fill the large room, deflated by her honesty.

"But there are still plenty more ships repair," she added.

"And even more in Bryn D'wall!" In this way, the young pilot sounded like his general.

Dannika nodded and made her way to the door.

General Klader was happy to continuously remind his troops, the king, and advisors to the throne, that the other side had more ships than them.

But he conveniently left out that most of theirs couldn't fly.

Assuming that was information his spies were privy to.

5

Dannika chewed on dried jerky in Renfro's workshop. She hadn't had time to make dinner, and by now it was late and her body was sore from the repair of the ship, she just wanted something to eat before bed. So jerky and hard bread it was.

And yet the work of the day still wasn't over. Not on a time crunch like this. And Dannika seemed to have less and less time every day.

Luckily this evening's work would be simple enough. She needed to contact a fellow wizard. After Renfro's death, Dannika was the last master wizard in Sithab. A few apprentices studied under her, specializing in the repair and maintenance of the ships, but she wasn't willing to take any of them on like Renfro had done with her.

Maybe because she didn't trust them. Maybe because they all seemed more enamored by Klader and his conquest than Renfro's ideals. Most likely because she didn't feel like a master of anything, let alone someone as wise as Renfro with knowledge to pass down.

Which led to lonely nights in the workshop eating dried meat and wondering how much longer until her head was on a block.

But Bryn D'wall had plenty of wizards, entire schools of wizards studying in classrooms, taking meticulous notes about the relics, and pushing the relic's abilities. Dannika had dreamt of sneaking over the Ragnar mountains, enrolling herself in their schools, becoming respected by Bryn D'wall's ruling council.

But that would be abandoning the people of Sithab, the people Renfro cared so much about.

So she settled for using the sending stone to contact Reagan, a wizard of Bryn D'wall.

The sending stone fit in the palm of her hand. It had strange pads on it like a dog's foot except a dozen of them instead of five. If she pressed them in the right order she was able to contact Reagan.

The sending stone made a trilling sound like a strange bird until Reagan answered.

Dannika had never met Reagan in person, but the pair had spent hours talking through the sending stones. Dannika trusted the wizard more than the apprentices who worked on the ships.

Any of those apprentices could've been bribed by Klader. Reagan, while their allegiance may be to Bryn D'wall, at least shared the same outlook on relics, their power, and their purpose as Dannika and her former master.

Once Reagan answered the pair exchanged pleasantries. Reagan seemed as exhausted as Dannika. Bryn D'wall had just as many problems as Sithab, if not more.

"Our scouts saw the crash yesterday," Reagan said. "Sorry that it didn't go well. How's the pilot?"

"He's fine, bailed from the ship in time not to get caught up in the flames. Repairs are exhausting and I have less than a week until the next, and maybe final, launch."

"Another in a week? We're lucky to get a chance to launch every month. Not that those go to plan," Reagan said. "We've done everything you've said and more. Still, no luck getting them in the air."

While there may be more wizards and ships in Bryn D'wall there were also more people on the ruling council. Instead of one king barking orders based on his advisors' suggestions, or occasionally not based on anything at all, Bryn D'wall had council after council after council to oversee the equitable management of the relics, along with food and land and other necessities.

The idea of getting a ship launched in a week was impossible in Bryn D'wall. And the slow process of trial and error was, in Reagan's view, the reason Bryn D'wall's ships were still on the ground.

But the slowness and multiple eyes on the ships had its advantages. Bryn D'wall had intricate documentation and an understanding of every part of the ship. So Dannika told her friend about the pilot's comment about the angels and how they protected him.

"Your pilot's comment is interesting," Reagan said clearly taking it more seriously than Dannika had.

"They're always talking about angels and demons," Dannika said with an exhausted groan.

"Well, we found something a while ago, small devices on the outside of the ship, coils of wire it seems. But they're all over the hull. When we disconnected them or damaged them, it caused the interior lights to turn off."

"What do you think they do? Control movement?"

"We couldn't tell, our ship wouldn't fly. But based on your pilot's report they may detect when something is nearby and adjust the ship's flight accordingly."

"And like most ancient technology it can think and react faster than a human."

"Not to mention they're facing every direction, countless eyes watching out for debris. We found some ancient texts referring to something called radar. I don't think these sensors are the same but they're similar."

"So this ship's radar must have been damaged?" It'd be one more thing for Dannika to check when reviewing if a ship was suitable for flight.

"Do you have anything for me?" Reagan asked. It was an unspoken rule from Renfro and Reagan's predecessor that equitable exchange of information was what kept these conversations viable.

Reagan had given Dannika a remarkable tip, one that might get Sithab through the debris field.

Unfortunately, Dannika had already shared all the technical knowledge she had with Reagan.

"Klader wants to attack Bryn D'wall soon," Dannika said. "The king is waiting until this next launch is finished."

"Then we hope it is a success," Reagan replied.

"I'm just not sure success will keep Klader at bay."

6

A sharp breeze, characteristic of Sithab's late fall, whipped Dannika's heavy robes in the wind. It had also pushed most of the clouds out of the sky. Leaving as clear a day as one could hope.

Dannika watched the debris float above her. Occasionally large pieces collided with each other and changed direction in the air. It was like watching clouds drift over a hill, except these clouds had taken down more ships than she cared to count.

The ship that Dannika and countless novice wizards had spent all week repairing sat in the middle of a large grassy field. The pilot, a young man who'd been up once before and was eager to go up again, climbed into the cockpit.

Despite the cold, the novice wizards were chattering about the launch. They were bunched together like sheep trying to make their own shelter from the wind. Dannika wondered if the group was genuinely excited to see the launch succeed, or were eager to get to work on dozens of other ships to prepare for Klader's invasion.

Dannika was glad to have someone with experience in the ship. She needed all the help she could get and she was willing to make a deal with angels, devils, or even a wild cat, to get the ship through the debris and back down again safely.

The king sat in a large chair on a wooden dais that'd been built to watch the launches. It had a roof to keep rain out, but right now she suspected the king wished it had sides to keep out the wind. The king was buried under a cloak that made him look like a bear ready for winter.

The king's carriage, a dozen horses, some with riders on them prepared to retrieve the ship in case of a crash were next to the dais, and tried to hide themselves from the wind with little success.

A dozen councilors, including General Klader and his right-hand man Galeb, stood next to the king. Their cloaks and jackets were tied tight. They spoke little and often in quiet murmurs that Dannika couldn't make out from her position on the field. They seemed unexcited to be out in the cold watching this launch.

Dannika was not excited either. A failure meant she'd be cut off from the project, a success meant a long winter of getting more ships in working order. And either way, Klader may invade Bryn D'wall.

The pilot gave the thumbs up showing all instruments, including the lights that indicated the radar angels, were operational.

Dannika turned to face the king who looked down at her. "With your permission sire, we are prepared to begin the launch," she said.

The king waved his hand uneager to let it out of his warm coat for longer than necessary.

The pilot lifted the ship off the ground. The red orbs turned a deep ruby color and a loud humming sound of their operation could be heard over the wind. Dannika smelled the burning grass, an uncomfortable smell that she'd come to associate with success, or at least hope.

It took no time at all for the pilot to get comfortable floating in the field and he took off to the sky faster than any pilot before.

The field was silent now that the ship was gone. Even the wind seemed to hold its breath in anticipation.

Dannika followed the path of the ship as best she could. But eventually, it shrank into a small metallic dot among a dozen pieces of metallic debris.

Dannika didn't know what success looked like, she'd been too focused on fixing the ship that she hadn't let herself imagine what a good outcome for today might be.

It would of course be the pilot coming down from the debris field in a controlled landing. Maybe the pilot would burn more grass as he brought it in for a landing.

Would she get the accolades and respect that her master had once had? Or would it, as she feared, just mean more long nights and an inevitable, unavoidable, invasion of Bryn D'wall?

Dannika didn't get to spend much longer dreaming about what success would be. Something came down from the debris.

It fell in the spiraling uncontrolled maneuver of a damaged ship. Something small broke free from the ship and she knew the pilot had ejected. The chaos of the crash was still too far away to be heard.

But she could hear Klader say something to the king.

Hoofbeats of scouts came next, tearing through the field.

Dannika couldn't do anything but stand still and watch the ship fall to the earth. She heard councilors climb on horses, the king called for his carriage and she heard the door shut behind him as it carried him off to the warm castle.

Klader stood next to her. Shouting orders to the novice wizards that had once helped Dannika repair the ship. "Begin unloading ships from storage. And start making preparations for launch."

Dannika doubted that Klader could name what one of those preparations would be but that was the luxury of being in charge.

The young wizards rushed to obey and he finally turned his attention to Dannika.

"I'm sorry that this didn't work, *wizard*," the word dripping with disdain. "But at least we can quit wasting valuable equipment on this endeavor."

Dannika watched the pilot float down to the surface under the canvas bag.

"Although it would have been interesting to see what weaponry we could find in the debris."

"If you're lucky you'll blow yourself up with it," Dannika said.

"I'm sure that Bryn D'wall will have plenty of new toys for us to play with. My sources say their wizard is very talented."

Dannika kept her mouth shut. She didn't want to give herself, or her friend Reagan away.

"I'm sure they'll be a spot for you as an apprentice, maybe the Bryn D'wall farmers need someone to scare the crows from their fields."

The pilot landed in the distance the canvas sack gently floated down and covered him and the chair. A scout rode out in that direction to help him.

"This afternoon I'd like you to bring every relic that might be helpful in this invasion to the armory," Klader said. "We will finally be using this technology as the ancients intended."

He marched off to bark orders at the young wizards before Dannika could come up with a retort.

Dannika would normally check on the pilot after a crash like this. But right now she didn't see the point. She wouldn't be able to act on any information the pilot gave her. Assuming the pilot didn't resent her for putting his life in danger once again.

She was done.

Done with this project. Potentially done as a wizard.

Klader's desire to have her revive ancient weaponry was no consolation.

Better to forget everything Renfro taught her than work against her master's wishes.

The icy wind seemed to freeze the tears on her cheeks. She hiked up the collar of her robes. It didn't do much to stop the wind, and it certainly didn't stop the tears.

The long walk to the workshop would give her time to get used to both.

To get used to the new reality.

7

Dannika latched the door of Renfro's workshop shut with a heavy wooden board. The wind would still find its way in through small cracks in the wall and gaps in the wood shutter window but that was the best she could do. And as per usual, the best she could do wasn't good enough.

Dannika immediately turned on the smokey crystal ball that sat in the center of the workshop. She'd debated whether or not she wanted to watch the crash the entire walk home. Now it just felt like the natural thing to do.

Not doing it would be admitting that the crash had failed, that she had failed, that Renfro was disappointed in her.

She was willing to put that off a little longer.

She was certainly willing to put off bringing ancient relics to Klader so he could figure out how to turn them into weapons.

The shoe-sized ship hovered above the green field. A few stacks of books towered over the ship. The miniature field was littered with a dozen giant tools. An ancient wrench, a screwdriver, a few sets of pliers. The ship didn't care about running into them, and neither did the miniature version of Dannika and the novices.

The ship took off, hovered just above Dannika's eyes, then started making its way through the debris that came down from the rafters.

The pilot did well to navigate the large pieces, the angels did the work they needed to so that he could avoid the smaller faster ones.

The pilot made it further than anyone else had before. Why hadn't he gotten through?!

The field became denser as the pilot got deeper into it. No one knew how thick it was, or if it ever ended. Ancient texts talked about there being space above them but maybe they filled all the space up with this ancient debris.

And as the field got denser Dannika realized what had caused the problem. Small pieces of debris, smaller than Dannika's thumb right now, but as big as a child in reality, knocked against the hull.

The angels couldn't guide the ship around them. There were bigger pieces to be worried about. It all moved too fast for the pilot to dodge, he was doing his best to avoid the pieces that dwarfed him like a house.

The child-sized pieces seemed inconsequential, at first. But slowly they dented the hull of the ship, then cut into it. The ship was strong, stronger than anything else made in Sithab. But it was likely the same material as the debris.

And they started destroying the hull.

The pilot was brave, determined, unwilling to turn back even though he should have.

A piece hit the crystal shell and shattered it, another cut a gouge in the top of the ship. Something hit a dark emerald thruster and the pilot lost control. Even the angels couldn't compensate for that.

The ship fell through the debris that it'd worked so hard to pass through. Dannika was surprised it didn't get caught up in the sea itself.

The ship fell out of the debris. The pilot ejected. But even in the green glow of the recording she could tell he was in bad shape.

Dannika turned the recording off in frustration. She didn't want to watch it again. What would there be to learn from it? She did everything she could to get the ship through the debris field. And that hadn't been good enough.

Dannika and her people would be stuck under this debris field, on this tiny little continent, forever.

A dozen wizards like Renfro couldn't get them through. And Sithab didn't even have one wizard like Renfro anymore.

Dannika threw some logs on the fire, considered throwing some books and delicate relics on it too in her frustration. She was at a loss for what to do next.

And for a while she did nothing. Stoked the fire, stared at the rafters, listened to the wind howl past the workshop. She chewed on a bit of bread but it felt hollow. She didn't have the energy to make a stew. For all she knew it'd burn up just like the ship.

The sending stone let out the strange bird-like trill that indicated Reagan was reaching out.

How was she going to tell her friend that Sithab would be invading soon?

"I'm sorry Reagan," Dannika said once the sending stones connected.

"We saw your launch," Reagan replied.

The foreign wizard's voice filled the room as if the wizard was sharing the workshop with Dannika, but Dannika was grateful she didn't have to face her friend in person.

"If you leave the capital you might be alright. They're only interested in the relics." Dannika knew that wasn't entirely true, but the further Reagan was from the border the longer they might survive.

"I won't be leaving," Reagan said with a determination that reminded Dannika of her master. "We have made progress with defenses."

"What happened?!" Dannika asked, knowing that this might be the last she ever heard about the ancient ships and their inner workings.

And, if Bryn D'wall had an advantage then maybe General Klader's failure would ruin the favor he had with the king.

"We triggered something by accident," Reagan said and their excitement was clear even over the sending stones. "An apprentice was working on something under the ship near the weapons and unexpectedly sparked something. The ship summoned an aura. It didn't hurt the technician and we weren't sure what it did because everyone could still approach the ship."

"Fascinating," Dannika said glad to have her mind on a new discovery.

"So we started hurling stuff at it. And the things we threw, tools, pebbles, bolts, they bounced off it like it was a wall."

"No way!" That was something Dannika had never witnessed or read about.

"When we threw stones slow they'd pass through but it shielded the ship from fast things."

"You said this was near the weapons, what did it look like?" Dannika asked eager to find this technology on one of her machines.

Reagan gave a response but Dannika couldn't hear it over the thud against the workshop's front door.

The workshop could hold up to the wind, it had for years.

What it couldn't hold up against was the two soldiers that burst through it in heavy armor.

Galeb, the general's right-hand man and hook-nosed spy waltzed in behind the soldiers, carefully stepping over the splinters that were once the door.

"Good evening Mrs. Dannika," Galeb said. "We're here to escort you to the king so you can stand trial in the morning."

"Trial for what?" Dannika asked. Sure she was supposed to bring relics to the general and had forgotten but that didn't mean a couple of guards and Galeb would show up to arrest her. Or at least it shouldn't.

One soldier took the sending stone out of Dannika's hand, the other pulled her hands behind her back and put cold metal manacles around her wrists. Reagan had likely cut the connection between the stones, without the right series of numbers it was just another useless relic.

"Right now the trial is to be about your misallocation of resources during a famine, and six counts of murder, potentially seven if today's pilot doesn't survive the night," Galeb said.

"I was acting under the king's orders," Dannika protested.

"I am quite interested in how that argument will go," Galeb remarked as if he were speculating on a joust.

The soldier handed the sending stone to Galeb who inspected it with feigned interest. "But now I'm interested in how you'll get out of treason and conspiring with the enemy."

8

The soldiers, probably different ones than the night before, led Dannika into the throne room where a small wooden platform had been erected for Dannika to stand on.

Her hands were still weighed down by shackles, although this time they were in front of her. Her robes hadn't been changed and were dirty from the night spent in the dungeon. Her grey hair was disheveled despite her best efforts to straighten it out with her fingers.

She looked more like a haggard witch than an archwizard.

The throne room was everything she wasn't. It was full of presentable people in the finest silks and most expensively embroidered robes. The ladies of the room, and likely a few of the lords, wore perfume that seemed to change with every step Dannika took past them. Citrus, rose, and lavender, all bombarded her nose. It was an improvement over the latrine smell of the dungeon.

Lanterns hung on the rows of columns that led to the king who sat on a raised platform in a polished metal throne. The throne itself had been recovered as a relic ages ago by the king's grandfather. It was likely part of some more complicated ancient device but the generations of kings seemed more interested in sitting on it than figuring out what it did.

"If it pleases you King Ramsey, the trial of Dannika Laskan will begin," said a young page standing at the foot of the throne.

The king gave a nod, almost disinterested in the trial before him. Even if he was as much, if not more, to blame for the actions Dannika took.

"The wizard Laskan is being charged with misallocation of resources, six counts of murder, and treason," the page continued. "General Klader is to begin with his explanation of accusations."

Klader stepped forward from the crowd of advisors that stood below the king's raised throne.

"Your sire, and his worthy advisors," he addressed the group he just came from. "The explanation should not be necessary. For years we have watched this wizard use and destroy military equipment, allocate capable men towards fruitless projects, and on six accounts let pilots go to the sky to die. This has cost the kingdom unimaginable resources and other opportunities like the chance to claim land and resources from Bryn D'wall."

Klader paused as a few of the advisors murmured among themselves. A few of the lords and ladies that lined the columned wall beside Dannika also spoke in hushed tones.

"And if that was all we might confine her if your Highness sees so fit. But my master of spies, Galeb, in the process of arresting Mrs. Laskan, found that she was using an ancient relic to communicate with an enemy wizard in Bryn D'wall."

Klader tried to continue but not very hard. The shocked murmurs of the crowd cut him off. He seemed pleased to let it continue. The king eventually cut the crowds off with a wave of his hand.

"Who knows how many secrets Mrs. Laskan may have shared with the enemy? If she is a spy loyal to them this entire time she might have been leading this counsel and our kingdom down a fruitless path.

"The only punishment this mortal council may offer to Mrs. Laskan is death. And we might hope that the gods exact revenge for the great nation of Sithab, and the people she's put in jeopardy, in the next life."

The council was silent a few nodding in agreement with Klader's comments. The general seemed content with his speech and stood next to the council. He did not take a seat.

"Mrs. Laskan may now make her defense," the page said.

They thought she was a spy? She was shaken to her core by that. She had never appreciated Klader, but she grew up in Sithab, she didn't want any harm to come to it. She was loyal to her master Renfro's mission to bring fortune to the people of Sithab. She'd never tell Bryn D'wall anything that might betray them.

Dannika was merely looking into the possibility of navigating the debris field so that all the great relics of the ancients that hung up there might help the kingdom, possibly help the whole continent.

Bryn D'wall was harmless, they had the same problem and Sithab and less magic. Not only that Reagan had helped Dannika achieve every success that Sithab had achieved. Although she could hardly tell that to the council.

"Mrs. Laskan," Klader said with an expectant look. "If you have no defense we can assume that you're guilty."

"I did not misallocate resources," Dannika began. Her words were hesitant and shaky as they came out as if even she wasn't unsure of the statement. "I was merely acting under the orders agreed upon by the council and your majesty. The pilots, whose deaths I mourn, flew the ships willingly. If I'm to be killed for these actions then all the rest of the council should suffer the same consequences."

"Myself and countless other council members tried to argue against your continued quest to launch ships and waste resources," Klader replied. "But when we stood against you you used your magic to turn our opinions and even the opinion of King Ramsey.

The rest of the council member nodded their heads in agreement clearly remembering a different course of events than her.

"We were only swayed to work against what's best for this country by your magical abilities."

"I don't have magic that can change someone's opinion," Dannika said dumbfounded by where Klader came up with that notion.

"Prove it," Klader said.

Dannika was stunned. She could see through the general's logical fallacies, any novice wizard could. But the room was not full of wizards. It was full of people looking for someone to blame so their own hides might be saved.

"If I had the ability to sway opinions wouldn't I use it here with my life on the line?" Dannika asked.

The courtroom murmured at this defense. They weren't in awe of the logic but instead sounded fearful of what tricks she might be playing on them.

"I can only assume that you don't have the power to sway this many minds. Or, more likely, my men were quick enough to catch you off guard so you couldn't prepare what you needed to."

"This is ridiculous," Dannika said, "I have no such magic and you have no proof that I do. I could just as easily claim that you're plotting to overthrow the king."

Shocked murmurs came from the audience.

"I am not the one on trial here. And the fact that the council has acted against their best intentions should be evidence enough."

"Then the weak spines of this council should be on trial."

Klader opened his mouth to continue but the king raised his hand silencing the entire throne room.

"The accusation of treason is enough to have you sentenced to death," King Ramsey said, his deep voice carried through the room with echoing finality. "And I have heard no defense or explanation against that accusation," the king said looking at Dannika with the intensity of an archer in battle.

Dannika swallowed her nerves. She'd hoped she had more time to come up with an argument but didn't get far.

"I have used the sending stones to communicate with Bryn D'wall. But–"

The room cut her off with a flurry of murmurs.

"But the Wizard Renfro," she spoke up to be heard above the crowd. "The Wizard Renfro believed the combined intelligence of wizards was the only way to decrypt the riddles of the artifacts. It's why he took on so many apprentices like me. The help we received from Bryn D'wall has helped us make it to the point of entering the debris field. With more help from–"

"Then this means Bryn D'wall's advice has enabled the death of six pilots and the injury of countless more," General Klader cut in.

Dannika ignored him making uncomfortable eye contact with the king, "the Wizard Renfro, was your trusted advisor for decades. He did not want this war. Using the artifact's weapons will destroy generations of work on both sides. A relationship can be built between wizards with the foundation of magic and that can broker relations between leaders. We can not live on this continent forever. Our youngest generations will have to take to the sky and escape the debris field like the creators of the artifacts meant to."

"Sire, we can not trust this wizard or any other to manage relations with Bryn D'wall. An alliance would be–"

The king lifted a hand to cut the general off. The general, and the rest of the room, were immediately quiet.

"You are correct, the Wizard Renfro was my trusted advisor, and I trusted his advice for years. However, times have changed and the world we live in now is different from the world Renfro studied in.

Your actions are inexcusable as an advisor. I sentence you to death. As an advisor, you have the ability to choose your method of execution."

Dannika's head raced. She was really going to be killed. Klader was going to start the war and use the ships to destroy the defenses of Bryn D'wall. She had the luxury of choosing her execution but she'd prefer not to have her throat strangled or sliced.

Dannika took a deep breath. It felt ridiculous but seemed a fitting method for her as a wizard and the criminal they had painted her to be.

"I would like to be put to death by the debris field."

The crowd murmured and Klader immediately protested while everyone in the crowd made their own remarks to each other.

Galeb whispered something in Klader's ear and Klader soon addressed the king privately in hushed tones.

The king waved his hand like he was casting a spell of silence.

"While this is unconventional and we need the resources for our upcoming invasion General Klader has advised me to graciously permit this."

Dannika was concerned that the general was on her side. But was grateful to at least have the chance to fly, and work on, a ship before her death.

"You have five days to prepare a ship," the king said. "Otherwise you will be hanged from the neck until dead."

9

Dannika looked up into the mess of wires, green boards of ancient components, and the former mounting brackets of the ship's weapon system. The aura system that Reagan mentioned had to be up here somewhere. She just didn't know what to look for. And there was a lot to look at.

The ship Klader had given her was in suspiciously good shape. The five novice wizards were remarkably competent and should be helping prepare the other ships for the invasion. Instead, they were running through diagnostics for Dannika's launch in the morning.

She doubted Klader had decided to show her mercy. But with the impending execution on her mind, she hadn't spent time figuring out why he would enable her now. Especially when he'd been so against the flights.

But her mind still drifted as she worked. She barely slept the past few days, it seemed pointless to sleep when there was work to be done and the tiredness would end with her execution.

Her mind drifted to Reagan and Bryn D'wall. How they might be preparing for the invasion. Dannika's silence was clearly not a good sign. Maybe the auras of their ships would be enough. She wondered if it would be enough to get through the debris field.

Dannika removed yet another piece of the weapon mounts. The ship was a dozen stone lighter without all the killing equipment installed.

Behind this mount was a silver metal cage. Twelve bars, as thin as twigs, held a ruby-red sphere inside of it. The cubed cage was just small enough to hold the ruby marble inside of it. Dannika had no idea how the ancients ever got the marble inside.

But remarkably enough it was captured inside the metal cube resting at the bottom of the cage. Whatever this was Dannika hadn't seen it before on another ship, although she'd never been allowed to remove this much weapons equipment.

It was amazing that she'd finally found something, something that might be part of the aura system. But who knew how difficult it would be to study it? And she had less than a day to do it. Would she be able to make it operational? How much magic might it need? Would the ship be able to power it?

She reached for a screwdriver to remove the cage being careful not to touch the ruby crystal and potentially shatter it. She reached behind the cube and to her amazement she found a dozen loose wires that terminated in a plastic connector.

Dannika felt around the back of the cage to see if there was a slot that might match these wire's connectors.

Sure enough, it did. She remembered being shocked as an apprentice at how many relics could be brought to life just by plugging wires in and feeding them enough magic.

The ruby marble began to glow. It floated into the center of the cubic cage small beams of laser light holding it in place.

Dannika shielded her eyes from the bright glow and dropped the screwdriver she'd been using to disassemble the machine.

A few of the novices cursed and one was so startled by the glow that he ran out of the room.

Dannika crawled out from under the ship and the entire room was tinted red. Two boys who were by the workbench inspecting the weapons systems out of curiosity looked at Dannika and the ship in awe.

How had Dannika tinted the whole room red? Was this how the aura was supposed to work? Or had she given it too much, or too little, power?

She walked towards the workbench and after a few steps, the room returned to its normal color of stone grays and white spotlights.

Dannika looked back at the ship and it had an egg-shaped red mist around it. She shouted in glee and excitement to get to see something so remarkable. This was the thrill and adrenaline that kept her committed to being a wizard.

But it was quickly doused by the sound of heavy boots entering the workshop from the large archway.

"I see that your advice to let the wizard tinker with one more ship has indeed proved fruitful," General Klader said to Galeb who silently walked next to him. The novice who'd fled the room when the aura first appeared padded along behind the two men.

"It will protect the ship from any damage according to the D'wallian wizard I overheard the traitor speaking to," Galeb said.

Klader stepped towards the shield and pounded his fist against it as he had done to the hulls a dozen times before.

His fist was not stopped by the shield.

"How is something as strong as mist going to protect a ship from arrows or ancient guns?" Klader asked.

Dannika was furious that she'd played into the general's hand. If she'd thought about it she would've known that the general would use whatever she discovered against Bryn D'wall. If she'd just agreed to be hanged he'd fly into Bryn D'wall without this aura to defend him. It'd give Reagan's people a chance to fight back.

But Dannika was incapable of putting a good puzzle down. Always had been.

Galeb walked over to the workbench where a few novices hovered looking in awe at the ship and its new discovery. He picked up a wrench and threw it as hard as he could at the ship.

The aura, sure enough, stopped the wrench and it fell to the ground outside of the egg-like shell.

Galeb smiled at the general, and it was as creepy as if a snake itself had learned to grin.

"The D'wallian wizard said it only stopped high-speed objects," Galeb explained. "The D'wallian wizards have enabled this on all their ships. Even if they don't fly they could mount the ships in strategic positions and shoot our ships down. And our weapons will do nothing to stop them."

"Unless we send in a few foot soldiers to destroy Bryn D'wall's ships by hand," the general said picking up on the hints his spy was giving him.

"So now we know how to fight them," Galeb said, "and we have as strong a defense as them."

"Show these apprentices how to enable this on all the other ships, wizard," Klader said.

"And if I refuse?" Dannika asked.

"Then I'll behead you myself," Klader said. "And these apprentices will figure out how to do it anyway. Do you really want to risk the ability to explore the debris as you've always dreamed?"

Dannika furrowed her brow. She could stand up to Klader here, but what good would it do? She'd already discovered enough. The first novice to crawl under the ship would see the ruby marble in its cage. Who knew how many other ships merely needed this system plugged into work? Or some minor repair to the cage, crystal, or wires.

And, with this aura on her ship, she might be able to get through the debris, come back with news and hope and opportunity for expansion to the sky, instead of to the east.

"Fine," the wizard relented.

"I knew you'd see it my way," Klader said. "I want this operational on all the ships by tomorrow afternoon," he said to the novices.

And even though that was clearly impossible not a single apprentice protested.

10

It was another cold and windy day on the launch field. A few dozen black patches from the thrusters of the ships that'd launched before littered the field around Dannika's ship.

Dannika stood in with the tight flight suit under the thick wizard robes. It all did little to keep the wind out. Her hands were manacled together and she stood at the base of the king's dais.

A remarkable crowd had formed around the king and in the field. Not just advisors and high-born lords but farmers and butchers and schoolchildren all of them interested in the wizard's remarkable execution.

General Klader seemed pleased with the turnout as he addressed the crowd and the high-born lords and the advisors of Dannika's misdeeds and treason. A warning to any others who might stand against him, or be sympathetic to the foreigners they were to wage war on.

"Any final words wizard?" the king asked from under the thick robes he wore.

"Everything I've done has been through the guidance and teaching of the Wizard Renfro," she had to shout to be heard over the gusts of winds. "In life, he believed in the wonder of magic and the hope it would bring. I only worked with Bryn D'wall to keep that hope alive. Hope that we may find prosperity in the ancient's magic, in their debris field. Something that will let us make the most of this small continent instead of having to squabble like mutts for scraps."

The crowd seemed disinterested in her words. It was difficult to be a pacifist on the eve of a war.

"I hope that instead of fighting with each other we might reach to the debris and find resources to escape this continent and maybe the planet as a whole."

The crowd did not cheer or murmur. They shivered in their boots huddled together to block out the wind. The king's eyes were as blank as ever. He waved his hand for the execution to start. Clearly eager for it to so he could return to his moldy castle.

Klader's guard unlocked her manacles. She walked to her ship. There was no ground crew of novices to guide her or help do pre-flight checks. No one expected her to go far. There was a young page holding a ladder against a ship and a half dozen horses ready to fetch the rubble, and her body when she returned to the planet.

Dannika moved through the preflight checks as quickly and thoroughly as possible. She had as much magic as the ship could store, the lights that held the angels glowed around her. The crystal dome was secured around her.

She pressed the control button to summon the aura around her ship.

That got a bigger reaction from the crowd than anything she'd done today.

With a deep breath, Dannika lifted off the ground. She couldn't smell it but she knew that grass was burning under her from the thruster's red-hot glow.

Dannika lifted off the ground like a hawk taking flight. Slowly she pulled away from the ground speeding up. The thrusters shifted behind her to give her more of a boost and soon small bits of debris that were low in the field pelted against the red aura that surrounded her making small white sparks like rain splattering against a window.

The debris field was thick with large pieces of ancient technology in no time. Dannika weaved through them as best she could dodging the biggest pieces herself, letting the angels jerk her out of the way of fast-moving horse-sized pieces.

She could see blackness between the gaps of the largest pieces. Small bolts and fist-sized sheets of metal hit the aura but were deflected without doing any harm to her hull. This was where the last pilot had failed. This is where she would be executed.

The aura held, even though the magic was draining fast from the ship. Soon enough it was only large pieces of cracked debris that looked like ships in their own right, albeit bigger than even the castle and far less sleek than Dannika's little ship.

Two spherical rocks hung above the planet. Moons as the ancients called them. But if they had a name it'd been forgotten to time.

The sun was brighter than she'd ever imagined it could be. It loomed in the distance no bigger than her thumb. But it sent nearly blinding rays of light at her. More hope than she could ever know what to do with.

Other than the sun and moons the sky was black, instead of the light blue that occasionally peaked through. Small pinpricks of light were scattered across the black canvas. She wondered what they were. The eyes of gods watching down on her? More debris to be escaped from? Small moons or suns that were remarkably far away? It all seemed unlikely, unbelievable.

She set her sights on the planet below, surrounded by gray debris. The planet, much like the moons and sun, was round. She could see the curved horizon, saw splotches of blue sea through the debris and patches of green land that humanity called home. It seemed so small compared to the sun and the moons and the planet as a whole.

Looking at the amount of magic still stored in the ship Dannika saw she was just over halfway through her supply. She could head back to the field, as other pilots would've done, she could let her magic supply run low, crash into some debris here. She could even fly to Bryn D'wall, give them one working ship, and be hailed as a talented foreign wizard. Assuming none of Klader's spies found her and assassinated her.

She had achieved what Renfro had always dreamed of. And he'd always dreamed of being able to bring the knowledge of the power of this technology back to the people of Sithab.

To follow her master so dutifully and then betray him, and her country, in the last moments of success didn't feel right.

She turned the nose of her ship to face the debris field and barreled towards it.

The large ships were easy enough to pass through. The angels helped guide her through the fast-moving bits of relics. The aura deflected the small bolts and fist-sized pieces. But every piece it deflected took more magic away from the ship.

Dannika saw a gap in the debris with a field below it. She made her way through it. The angels tried to push her right and left at the same time to make it through the closing gap. Neither was successful and the large pieces collided into the aura using up the last of its magic reserves. The red field she looked through disappeared and she saw the stark green field below her. The debris closed in on her, hit the tail of her ship, and knocked her off course. She heard the small pieces of debris hit her hull and crystal dome-like hail against stone paths.

She fought to control the ship, to not crash it like the dozens of pilots before her. She considered ejecting but knew that'd be a betrayal of the system of execution she'd chosen.

She pulled against the stick that controlled the ship and finally got the beast under control and hovered it above the grassy field.

The king's dais was a speck on the horizon she'd come down a little south of where she'd launched.

On her way back to the field she passed the horsemen scouts who were prepared to recover the crashed ship. Dannika passed them too fast to take in the shocked look on their face.

Dannika landed the ship, its magic reserves nearly exhausted. She opened the hatch of the cockpit and waited for someone to bring her a ladder.

The only thing happening in the silent windy field was Klader and the king discussing this matter quietly.

Finally, under the king's orders, a large guard brought Dannika a ladder and escorted her to the king, this time not in manacles.

"You have survived the detritus field," the king said and it sounded like a mix of a question he couldn't ask because of his position."

"I have Your Majesty. There are countless artifacts and materials we could harvest to improve our lot, sire," Dannika replied.

"While you are no longer an advisor on my council I will take your observation into consideration.

"Am I to be executed now, sire?" Dannika asked unsure of her standing.

"The fates have seen fit to spare you and I am not about to anger them on the eve of a war," the king said. "I forbid you from practicing magic or holding any position of power. You will be confined to the castle grounds so that your knowledge will not fall into the hands of Bryn D'wall."

And true to his word the king made room for Dannika in a small room in a western tower. She was as disregarded as a mouse or a stubborn patch of mold in the grout.

She was banned from the library and ancient relics were kept at a distance from her, as if her gaze could set them off. Rarely did a novice wizard, or an advisor ask for her advice or guidance. When it did happen got limited news of the war. It didn't sound promising for Bryn D'wall but the war wasn't kind to the king's resources.

Dannika spent her time painting and drawing remarkable images of the world above. She was a novice, at first, and was constantly striving to capture the wonder she'd seen above the debris field.

Each painting kept the fragile thread of hope alive, that one day, someone would look at her pictures and see a horizon worth pursuing.

Invisible Corridors

Expansive blue sky and dusty brown plains stretched as far as my eyes could see. Soft orchestral background music played as three dozen procedurally generated faces crowded me and grunted to me in their unintelligible language.

Maybe it was a thank you. More likely it was a fuck you. The devs left that to our imagination.

I distributed the bounty of this season's harvest to the NPCs. The harvest hadn't been great, pests wiped out most of it. Everything I was planning to sell to the traveling merchants. It left me with a choice: money or more workers for next spring.

In real life, I'd always wondered what the point of breeding was. In this game, it was clear: Get more workers, better resources, automate any process I didn't want to do. Eventually, reach the stars and win the game.

Humanity had succeeded. Yet they still played the game. Spawning resentful characters like me.

The NPC villagers took the simulated food and ran off to their huts. Soon there would be four and a half dozen procedurally generated faces and hopefully, the upcoming year's harvest would be bountiful. I'd know soon. In an hour another year in the game would pass.

Maybe one day with my guidance this civilization would have brick houses instead of huts. Assuming a plague or storm or act of god didn't wipe it out. That was the way the civilizations of my last few play-throughs had ended. In tiny, pixelized graves.

"Dewey, did you take out the trash?" my mother called from the other room.

I could barely hear her over the background music of the game. Left me with another choice. I could ignore her. But then this run would be ruined by something worse than an act of god. An act of mom. Can't advance them to brick houses if the console is taken away.

"I'll get to it later," I called back.

"Get to it now."

Avoid responsibility or face it. Based on my conversation with Erika at school today this wouldn't be the last time I would face that choice tonight.

I paused the game and pulled off the headset. The village shrank to pixels behind the glasses. Blue sky and dusty plains were the only things visible in the thumb-sized lenses.

Windowless metal walls of my interior cubby surrounded me. Posters and pictures were held to the walls with magnets. We'd advanced past clay huts. Metal walls kept the vacuum of space out, far more dangerous than a roaming lion. But was it really a privilege to live in a closet?

On top of the mess of the desk my hand terminal sat. I checked it. Still blank. No news was good news. Despite that, I didn't let out a sigh of relief.

Responsibility always found you. Even if you were in the invisible corridors of the station where the security cameras were painted over. It'd find you eventually.

Didn't keep me from wanting to avoid it.

Clothes cluttered the floor and the coffin-sized bed was unmade. Two more chores my mother would nag me about if she came in. I took the clear path across the small room to keep that from happening.

The living area of the apartment still smelled like dinner, rehydrated chicken and broccoli. It smelled as uninspiring as it had tasted. My mom sat on the couch staring at her hand terminal, she hardly looked up.

Dinner became more pungent, along with a half dozen other past meals, as I pulled the sack out of the trash can. I could ask my mother why she didn't do this herself, but I already knew the response: "Raising you is my chore, and you don't make it easy."

Dragging me into this world, the chore that would end all other chores. After nine months and a few dozen diapers, there'd be someone to take out your trash, wash your dishes, and visit you in a nursing ward in your old age.

I hauled the trash bag at arm's distance as my bare feet padded against the cool metal floor of the station's hallway. I dodged the small trickle of soda that now leaked out of the bottom. I resented myself for throwing it in there still half full a few days ago. I resented that they made these bags so thin.

Someone else's kid would have to take care of that chore. Some kid whose father raised him to be a janitor so he could raise his kid to be a janitor too. Like morticians and doctors, every station needed a janitor.

The bag disappeared down the waste chute. I hoped I could disappear into my room just as easily.

No luck.

"Did you put a new bag in?" my mom asked before I got to my bedroom door.

I groaned but headed back to the kitchen.

I tucked the sides around the rim neatly, just like Dad wanted me to do it. A carbon copy of him doing things the meticulous way he wanted them done. Skipping a step would earn me a lecture that was twice as long as it took me to do it right.

We correct you because we care.

I wish you didn't do either.

What would I teach my kid? How to play video games and duck my responsibilities? Sure, there was an art to it, just no money. And I wasn't even that good at it. I took care of my responsibilities when it came down to it.

Would I teach him where the invisible corridors are? Where they paint over the security cameras because teenagers need to have a place to get away from their parents and be their own person.

"Have you seen your grades for this semester?" my mother asked once the bag was in place.

I certainly wouldn't be teaching the kid math.

"What are you going to do about this? You need to ask your teacher for extra credit. Your father won't be able to get you an internship in his terraforming lab with grades like this."

"Lucky me."

"What was that?" But she barreled on without waiting for me to clarify. "I'm messaging your teacher. You're going to do whatever extra credit he assigns."

I slouched off to my room.

"It isn't easy raising you," followed behind me.

I didn't see how that was my fault.

Why did my parents want me to be like them? Didn't they see the bummer their life was? They probably couldn't tell. Otherwise, they wouldn't get out of bed in the morning.

But they were as proud to have me as I was of some of my high scores and speed run times. They'd worked just as hard at it too.

I'd be an old man before I quit hearing about how my conception was a miracle. That surviving the premature birth was remarkable. Even if it didn't feel remarkable that I was shorter than the guys that pushed me around in school.

If my dad wasn't working late I'd hear statistics about how bad infant mortality rates are on the stations. How they're nearly as high now as they were on old Earth.

That was a glitch that would be reported to devs and patched immediately. Otherwise, it'd be exploited by the players.

Maybe they'd exploit it by linking fertility care to employment so that even the toughest jobs were filled. Just so that the player's already insanely high score would go up or the game might be won a second or two faster.

No. That was too close to reality for a video game.

The hand terminal on my desk was no longer blank. Erica's message sat there. Waiting to be delivered.

Maybe they painted over the cameras and never cleaned them off, because younger women had more success carrying a baby to term. Yet another exploited game mechanic.

The point of breeding was clear. More workers meant more work was done. Upgrade the clay huts to brick houses to metal space stations. Mine the resources of the planet below so that we could afford rehydrated food and thin trash bags. Terraform it so my children might walk under a blue sky that wasn't simulated.

What player was this serving? Certainly not the ones doing the work.

It wasn't that I didn't want to be a dad. I'd enjoy it if I wasn't so aware of how bad the world I brought the kid into was. Maybe whoever designed this world should've focused on making it somewhere worth living. Then I might even look forward to fatherhood.

I'd settle for imperfect. No game is without its bugs, risks, and glitches. I just didn't like playing games that were rigged against me.

"I got the test back," Erika's message said. "We should talk."

Responsibility always finds you. Even in the invisible corridors where the security cameras are painted over.

A Sip of the Real Stuff

Humans used to know that the underworld opened up on All Hallows Eve. That demons and ghosts and zombies and things spookier than mortal imagination could ever conceive were free to wander past the borders of their nightly haunts that Halloween night.

Their ancestors made it impossible to forget. They built dozens of different memorial holidays across dozens of different cultures to mark the event into humanity's memories.

Yet something still got lost in translation.

Spooky things became cheap costumes. The treats were for the kiddos, not bribery to keep the ghouls at bay. The tricks turned into harmless egging or maybe some frustrating toilet paper in the trees.

But that didn't stop people like Alina from walking among the humans on that night.

Which is how Alina found herself hugging a wall near the edge of the room sipping something far too weak and too sweet to be considered a cocktail. It tasted of fake strawberry syrup and hardly had a bite of alcohol behind every sip. But it gave her something to do with her hands as the crowded party raged on around her.

She'd been attending this party for nearly a decade. It was hosted in a New York brownstone. The house was decorated with imitation cobwebs that would be dusted off by the maid within minutes any other time of the year. The owner was so rich he didn't care who showed up. She didn't know any other guests either, they weren't her typical company. But that was the beauty of showing up unannounced on this special Halloween night.

She listened to a man in a shirt that read "Error 404: Costume Not Found" in big block letters explain why this whole holiday was overrated, over-commercialized, and just an excuse for corporate interests to sell more sugary candy and pumpkin-spiced drinks. She agreed with him on some points, but just like the rest of humanity he missed the mark in the end.

What hadn't missed the mark this evening was the intricacies of the other party goer's outfits. There was a sharp-toothed clown with frizzy electric blue hair, a pair of cowpokes, a fellow in an inflatable

T-rex costume, and a dozen other well-thought-out get-ups. Mr. 404 was an exception, along with the one woman wearing scrubs and a stethoscope, there was a chance she'd just gotten off work or was on call to return in case of an emergency.

Alina had hardly put in any work tonight, but she didn't have to. The skin's face was warped and marred as if she'd been badly burned. It pulled her cheeks down into an expression that seemed like she was on the brink of letting out a ghastly scream. Any other night she'd be stared at uncomfortably, she wouldn't dare go out like this in the sunlight. But on Halloween night she was free to go where she pleased getting compliments on her intricate makeup.

But she didn't have to use any makeup to make her skin ghostly white. She never bought fancy contact lenses to make her irises as blue as arctic glaciers. Her dress, a tattered navy-blue thing that billowed at the faintest hint of a breeze, was not purchased at some pop-up Halloween store. No prosthetic mask made her nose look as flat and open like a skull; her cartilage had decayed ages ago.

She might be the only genuine person here.

The room smelled like buttery pumpkins and other roasted treats; their scents stronger than the alcohol in Alina's drink. Some creepily themed hors d'oeuvres that the host was serving the guests. Pigs in a blanket that looked like severed fingers, deviled eggs that looked like the unholy eyes of Satan himself, and fine white cheeses cut into cute little ghosts that were a far cry from the actual thing.

Music played over a speaker. Some song that vaguely related to the holiday. There were never any songs specifically written for the holiday, not like Christmas carols that lasted for centuries. But humans found a way to link their favorite songs into this holiday nonetheless.

Alina hardly talked at these events. She was happy to lean on a wall hold a drink and watch the fascinating characters around her. It was a nice difference from the mourners that loomed around her usual haunting grounds. Groups of people broke out in laughter around her and the bell-like jingle of their laughs juxtaposed their creepy masks.

But every once in a while, there was someone brave enough to walk up to her. Usually, some misguided or intoxicated buck that assumed her face was a mask and could be taken off with enough charming talk.

So, she wasn't surprised when a man in his mid-forties walked up and introduced himself as Roland. His face and hands were painted a crimson red, his lips were black as coal. He saved some effort on body paint by covering his broad chest with an old-fashioned three-piece suit. The suit was as black as his hair except for a little scarlet handkerchief in his breast pocket and a matching red bow tie. His cleft chin seemed to jut out from under his mouth like a beak. It was adorned with a jet-black soul patch that was hardly bigger than one of Alina's overgrown and cracked fingernails. Curls of messy black hair was receding back from his forehead but he'd made the best of his aging hairline and mounted two swooping horns on the bald patches.

The horns were magnificent, in Alina's professional opinion. They weren't a polished plasticky black like most costume horns were. Roland's horns had superficial ridges in them just like the horns of a ram or goat or demon. They swooped back behind his head like a branch bent by heavy winds.

His eyes were black as if the pupil had dilated to the point of hiding the rest of the eyeball. A single golden ring, that seemed to glow, gave away the direction he was looking. And he was looking at her face taking in her "costume" as much as she was taking in his. Either this man had the misfortune of actually seeing a demon at some point in his life or had a remarkable imagination.

"Are you enjoying my party?" he asked.

Well, that explained it. If he could afford a party like this, he could certainly afford professional makeup as a costume. He could also probably afford to serve drinks that were stronger than a geriatric squirrel.

"It's the best time I've had out all year," she answered honestly, having to look up at him since he was about a head taller.

"I try not to disappoint. People travel long distances to enjoy it." Roland's voice was deep, he had a hint of a New York accent mixed with something else Alina couldn't quite place. "I think there's a fellow that came here from hell itself, or maybe he drove in from New Jersey."

"Well, I hear traffic can be Jersey trying to get out of hell this time of night," Alina replied.

Roland let out a deep chuckle to that. His teeth were glistening white, especially compared to his crimson red skin. They also seemed to be costume dentures with unnaturally sharp incisors.

Alina didn't want to like him. She wanted to shrill and screech and scare him away like she would to any other mortal any other night. She knew he was disingenuous, like every other costumed person at this party. There were a dozen women within earshot that were dressed in less than her and had put on make-up with the intention of impressing, instead of having a face made to scare people away.

Unfortunately, Roland seemed intent on talking to her. "Are you from around here?" he asked.

Boring small talk that wouldn't charm a drunken Labrador. "Grew up around four o'clock on the third circle of Hell," she said, hoping something genuine would throw this devil for a loop.

"Talk about growing up on the wrong side of the tracks. You never stood a chance." Like a catcher, he wasn't even startled by the curve ball. Impressive.

Alina took a sip of her drink trying to think of something that might scare him away. It was much harder when she couldn't use a deafening shriek. She could explain the political inner workings of Hell to the mortal. She could tell him how his claim she'd grown up in a bad neighborhood was correct. But she didn't want to give him the satisfaction.

"They're weak aren't they."

"Pardon?" She didn't like being caught flat-footed.

"The drinks. You'd think I'd be able to serve something with some kick to it. But I've had rum cakes with more liquor in them."

"And the syrup tastes like a freshly dug grave," she said pushing her drink into his hand. She noticed his nails were black like his horns plus they were clipped short and polished smooth. "Where's the real stuff hidden?" she asked. At least a little interested in seeing what it might take to catch this Roland fellow off guard.

She drifted up the stairs behind him as he led her to a library on the second floor of the house. She'd wandered in here a few years before; it hadn't changed a bit. There hadn't been a speck of dust then and there wasn't one now.

Two windows looked down on the busy street below. It was too late for children to be trick or treating but like any other night in New York, there were people wandering the streets. Some might be looking to pull a trick on someone, others might have valuable treats for the tricksters in their satchels and backpacks.

An old grandfather clock that sat between the windows chimed a warning that it was a quarter to midnight, its pendulum swung back and forth with consistent click. On each side of it, in front of the windows, sat two leather armchairs. They were a rich burgundy red. Roland walked between them and cracked open a beige globe which hid a few bottles of liquor inside. The whole room smelled like old books and old leather, an exotic smell that seemed to wrap Alina up in a hug.

A large wooden desk sat in the middle of the room looking at the windows, a comfy leather chair with buttons covering the back, and a seat with divots sat behind the desk. The three other walls were covered in floor-to-ceiling bookshelves apart from the door they'd entered in from.

Alina drifted around the room her feet barely making a sound on the hollow second floor. She perused the books that were at her eye level. Some were tattered and old others had shiny dust jackets protected by thin plastic. It was shocking the floor of this place didn't fall out from under the weight of the countless books. The most remarkable thing about the books was that they didn't have any titles. The only thing on the spines was the author's name.

"Any of these worth reading?" Alina asked when she'd drifted back over to Roland who handed her a real drink.

"A few," Roland replied, "but not nearly as many as you'd think." He clinked the rim of his glass against hers and took a sip.

She followed suit. The scotch he'd poured tasted like peat moss, a foreign kind of dirt that American graves never had. It was exotic, exquisite, and enjoyable. She swallowed the rest of it in excitement. She wouldn't get drunk but she'd certainly enjoy the flavor.

"Careful," Roland said stepping forward and pulling the red handkerchief out of his breast pocket. "You spilled some on your neck."

Alina let out a frustrated blessing. She didn't drink often enough to remember the small hole in her neck. The one that whistled like a flute when her lungs really got going. She took the handkerchief and turned away to clean herself up.

"What do you do for work?" she asked in an attempt to distract him.

"Talent acquisition," he replied leaning on the desk with a creek.

"Like an agent?" she asked, assuming he was focused on writers considering the large library.

"More or less."

This guy might genuinely be a devil, but at least the job explained the ridiculously expensive house. "Do you enjoy it?"

"Honestly?" he asked as if he wasn't sure she could handle his sincere opinion.

"Is there else anything worth being?" she asked.

"Honestly, I am a bit over it. I got transferred to New York ages ago hoping the influx of European immigrants might make acquisitions interesting. And don't get me wrong the mafia followed by the lawless 80s as a whole were interesting but more evil is done online now than anywhere else and it really takes the fun out of pounding the pavement for good old-fashioned talent. Now I'm stuck in this blessed city. I couldn't go to Jersey if I wanted to."

"A lot of these books written by mafia men?" Alina asked turning her attention back to the shelves.

"Odds are good anything that sounds like it was written by a dago or mick was a mobster at one point. What about you? Do you enjoy your work?"

"Sure, when it comes my way. But not a lot of people come by anymore."

"What do you do?"

"Reception," Alina replied. Then feeling she wasn't being particularly genuine either added, "for a graveyard."

"Ahh," Roland said sounding like he understood. Clearly, he was so rich he'd never visited a graveyard without a receptionist. He finished his scotch and poured another glass for the both of them.

"People just don't mourn like they used to." He handed the glass to Alina who sipped it carefully this time. "Used to be I throw a trolley problem at someone and they commiserate their decision for days. Now they're all so analytical. They pull the switch and move on with their lives."

"Sure, yeah, exactly," Alina sputtered out trying to make sense of his words. Normally she could tell when people were messing with her but Roland, with his costumed face, was difficult to read. He seemed genuine but he didn't talk like any mortal she'd ever met. "No one visits graves after dark they just look up memorials online. If I do get a batch of kids in after dark, they whip out their phones before I can start wailing at them. And getting caught on camera is bad for business, takes the mystery out of it."

"You ever wish you could just pack it all up, move on, give up your line of work?" Roland asked leaning on the big wooden desk once again.

Alina followed suit, floating up slightly to sit on the neat surface of the desk. From this position, she was at his height, instead of being a head shorter than him. Being so close to Roland she caught what must've been his cologne. It was sweet like fermented fruit but also had a hint of something sulfuric as brimstone.

"Would that I could but what else am I going to do? Where else is there to go?" Alina asked. "I live for nights out like tonight but Halloween only comes once a year."

"You need to talk to your union rep about getting more days off," Roland said with a chuckle.

His black lips were turned in a grin but Alina just let out a sigh that caught the hole in her throat and made a disappointed whistle. Then the constant tick of the grandfather clock's pendulum filled the silent room. If she'd been more disappointed by his dismissive joke Roland would be deaf right now.

She'd thought she'd met someone that understood her. Someone that was as tired of the old way things were done as she was. She'd forgotten this was some rich man in a costume, as fake as everyone else downstairs.

"It's getting late. I should go." She put her glass down and floated off the desk.

"Wait," Roland said. His big red hand grabbed her bony-thin wrist. She slipped through his fingers like the ethereal being she was. He didn't seem to mind and pushed up his sleeve to check the time on a large golden watch. His flesh was red under his cuffs, and his white shirt didn't have any red paint smudges. Whoever had done his make-up was surprisingly neat and remarkably thorough.

"We've got a few more minutes until midnight," he said. "It took me nearly a decade to get up the nerve to talk to you. I'd hate to have to wait until next year to continue our conversation. Where can I find you?"

"You don't want to find me," Alina said, looking away from him towards the window. "This isn't some mask you can peel back and find something more interesting underneath."

"I never thought it was. But you're someone that is more interesting the more your defenses are lowered."

"Yeah well, it's not shocking that I've got a few defenses."

"I'd be shocked if a banshee like you was defenseless."

Alina turned to look at Roland who was standing surprisingly close to her. It made her nervous, made her want to flee out the door, back to her safe graveyard stomping grounds. But it also made her curious.

She reached out to pull on Roland's scarlet bow tie. It easily came loose. The first few buttons of his collared shirt easily came loose too. His chest was crimson red just like his hands and face.

"This isn't just some face paint you can wash off," Roland said.

"No. I suppose it isn't," Alina said staring at the crimson-red skin in front of her.

"We're stuck in this blessed city. Stuck on this mortal plane. It's outgrown us yet we can't escape it. But maybe we wouldn't need to escape it if we had each other."

Alina floated up to meet Roland's gaze. His black eyes and golden-ringed irises used to be impossible to read. But now that she knew she was looking at a devil she knew how to read him.

The determined wrinkle around his horns, the sustained golden glow of his eyes, and the thin grin on his black lips told her he had said a lot of genuine things tonight and that he honestly wanted to spend more time with her.

Alina leaned in and kissed Roland. Her twisted lips wrapped around his and it took a moment for him to register her kiss and react. His lips were fiery hot, a stark contrast to her ghoulishly cold lips. Her neck whistled in excitement as she sighed in delight. She'd unexpectedly connected with someone genuine tonight, even if it was just a brief sip of something real.

Then Roland did something unexpected and pushed her away.

Holding her ethereal body at arm's length he said, "There's fifty-eight cemeteries in New York—sixty-six if you count Staten Island—which one can I find you in?"

She started to tell him but the grandfather clock between the burgundy armchairs struck midnight, and even her loud banshee screams could be heard over its toll. She was pulled out of Roland's arms and across the city to her graveyard stomping grounds.

She let out a high-pitched frustrated scream that upset every dog in the city. Then she took a deep breath that whistled in her throat.

Fifty-eight cemeteries weren't too many to search. At one a night he'd find her before New Year's. Then every night would be an escape from this blessed city.

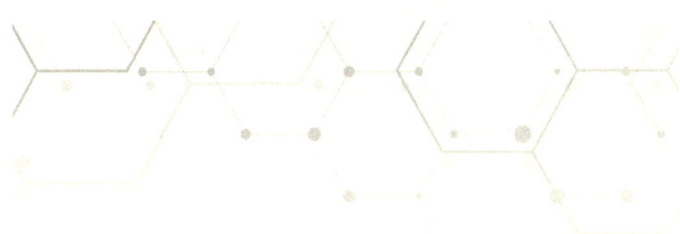

Aldren's Abandoned Station

F eldman's Station was quiet despite it being Elder's Day. The once-crowded station had, like most of the Central System, cleared out. They hadn't gone anywhere in particular, but like humanity as a whole began to disappear, falling prey to the beasts humanity had awoken.

Aldren, a teenage girl with matted-haired and a patched-up jump-suit that smelled like an algae vat left to grow on its own, had made Feldman's Station her home.

Or at least the parts of it that hadn't been sealed up due to breaches in the hulls. Those sectors had lost atmosphere and let in the deathly vacuum of space. Or worse, the things that lingered there.

Aldren couldn't leave Feldman's if she wanted to. The last ship had left months ago. It had carried a small crew of nomadic humans who jumped from outpost to outpost looking for surviving humans.

Feldman's was a common stop on those trips. It'd been famous for ages, popular enough to show up on the most outdated of nav systems.

Aldren was celebrating Elder's Day in style. She'd booked a table at Sunflower's Muse, one of the nicest restaurants still in atmo.

It wasn't hard to get a table.

The difficult part was finding a suitable meal. Anything fresh had molded before Aldren was born. The hydroponic vats still grew plenty of algae, but algae stew, chili, or soup was not a meal fit for Elder's Day. Most freeze-dried meals had been pillaged by Aldren and others who traveled to the station, leaving the already thin reserves dry.

But residents, former residents, of Feldman's Station had stashes. Aldren had sorted through countless bedrooms, personal belongings, and prized valuables. Most of which were useless to Aldren, hence why they were still on the station.

But in a nook under a bed, a freeze-dried ration had fallen and been forgotten. Until Aldren rescued it.

The vacuum-sealed zip t'lock foil bag was filled was beef stroganoff. Aldren hadn't had real beef and she didn't expect that to be changing today. This packet certainly held the vegan beef substitute.

Aldren poured the dried noodles, beef, and sauce flakes into a shallow white bowl. She'd picked this one out because it had the least number of chips in it. She poured hot water over the food to rehydrate it.

The room was immediately filled with the savory smell of beef and rich mushroom and onion sauce. A massive improvement from the salty green vegetable smell of algae chili.

Aldren listened to the Elder Day tunes she'd programmed into the station's public address system. The songs were upbeat and celebratory And would stick in your head for days after hearing them.

Other tables in the restaurant were set with muted yellow tablecloths and green napkins folded like hats. It'd taken a full day to do that, but Aldren wanted to keep the illusion that she wasn't alone on Elder's Day.

A present, wrapped in crinkled but shiny tin foil, sat across from Aldren. It stood out on the yellow tablecloth. She'd found something else useful in her pursuit of a good meal. And wrapped it for herself.

The beef stroganoff would take time to rehydrate. The best way to pass that time was to open the present.

Aldren carefully peeled back the plastic electrical tape, she didn't have much left. She unfolded the crinkled foil, which likely couldn't be used for much more in its life, but you don't survive on an abandoned space station by wasting supplies. The small cardboard box was easy to open. Aldren hadn't wasted tape keeping it closed.

She pulled out a mismatched pair of neon socks. They were long like a tube. One was pink with a blue patch on its toe and heel, the other was blue with a pink patch on the toe and heel.

The socks were absolutely gorgeous! Exactly what Aldren wanted.

She wrapped her arms around her chest and gave herself a warm hug. Another thing you had to do if you wanted to survive on an abandoned space station.

The stroganoff was as hydrated as it would be. Aldren knew there'd still be crunchy dehydrated bits in it. But that was the charm of freeze-dried meals, algae stew had no texture.

As she stirred the stroganoff around the public address system announced: "New ship docked in sector gamma partition C door 12."

Aldren had wired the station's security into the PA to keep from having to go through vacuumed sectors to access the station's security office. She'd also programmed the security feed to transmit directly to her hand terminal.

Aldren's heart sank. Unfortunately, she had guests for Elder's Day.

You don't survive long on an abandoned space station by getting excited about having company.

Sector gamma was mostly still in atmo. Lucky for the new ship. Some travelers docked into vacuum, no lack of hassle.

On Aldren's hand terminal, a feed of the sector gamma's security camera played. The image was focused on the door the ship docked to. The ship itself was ocean blue, not that Aldren had ever seen a real ocean. Harbor Master was painted in blocky white letters on the side. The ship as a whole was sleek like a knife or pair of needle nose pliers.

It was probably designed to land on planets and had to get through the heat of a planet's atmosphere.

Apparently, the operator of the Harbor Master was also not eager to have company. They hadn't opened the doors of the dock or made an appearance in the station yet.

Or if they had the cameras had missed it.

Another thing Aldren didn't appreciate.

An abandoned station had no security team to actively prevent hacking the camera feed. The simple security measures that Aldren could put in place were outdated and easy to bypass.

She took a bite of the stroganoff. She looked around and appreciated the neat grid of tables she'd laid out together in Sunflower's Muse. Keeping one eye on the terminal and another on her spoon, not wanting to spill a bite, she did her best to enjoy her Elder's Day meal.

If Aldren's visitor wasn't eager to see her, then she wasn't eager to see them.

Besides, not every human that visited Feldman's was friendly. But the station's booby traps would keep them out of Aldren's living quarters.

A snap rang through the Sunflower's Muse. It sounded like a circuit breaker blowing. Aldren dropped her spoon and splattered sauce all over the yellow tablecloth.

The smell of ozone, another clear sign of an electrical problem, filled the room.

Aldren grabbed her socks off the table. A fire in her station could be deadly. She knocked her chair over in her haste and turned around to make it to the door.

Unfortunately, a large toothy beast blocked her path.

The Awakening, caused by greedy Central System scientists if you believed the myths, let monsters into this universe through the space between space.

Some monsters were like whales and swam through the void of space swallowing ships whole. There were jellyfish-like creatures orbiting suns and placing their tentacles on the hot stars when they were hungry and casting the whole solar system into darkness once they were full.

The creature in front of Aldren had fur as black as the void of space. It stood on four legs and had triangular feline ears.

It seemed like a jungle cat, maybe a panther. And just like she'd seen in VR videos this panther had a short muzzle, muscular shoulders that reached Aldren's chest, and four tails that floated behind it.

Except Aldren didn't think panthers were supposed to have bulbs on the end of their tails. These bulbs, which only existed on three of the four hovering tails, twisted open like a flower blooming. Each was filled with an array of suction cup-like tendrils. Then they closed in the reverse motion, only to repeat the cycle a moment later.

On second thought, Aldren wasn't sure that panthers were supposed to have four tails at all.

"Hello," the panther said in a deep voice that seemed to shake the whole station. "What do you have there?"

The panther's yellow eyes with their inhuman vertical slits gazed at the socks in Aldren's hands.

Aldren buried the socks in the pocket of her jumpsuit.

"Nothing," she said rushed.

She had no gun, those were dangerous on a station. A multitool was strapped to the work belt of their jumpsuit, but the small blade would be as useful as the stroganoff-covered spoon.

"It's Elder's Day for you humans. Is it not?" the panther asked.

"Mhmm," Aldren said nervously. She backed away, uneager to get within paw's reach of the beast.

The beast kept up with Aldren's retreat. For every few steps back she took the panther caught up with a single stride.

Beasts like this didn't get the label of monster by being kind to humans.

"Isn't it tradition to give gifts to others on Elder's Day?" the panther asked.

"Of course," Aldren responded. "You can have..." she looked around the room and snatched a neatly folded green napkin off of a nearby table. "...this," she said holding the gift out.

The panther frowned, as much as a feline-faced extra-dimensional being could frown.

"There's no love or warmth in that gift," the panther complained.

"I folded it myself. For you," Aldren said. She pinched and pulled the edges making sure the folds were sharp and neat.

"They didn't want to give me a gift on the Harbor Master either," the panther said.

Aldren hummed in interest and concern for herself.

"They shot at me, trapped me, lopped off part of my tail."

The panther lowered the three tails that had pulsing bulbs on the ends. It was clear to Aldren that the fourth one had been cropped a bit short.

"But there was warmth and love in the family's ship. So I kept that as a gift. And I kept its course. Which led me to this station."

The panther smiled the kind of cruel smile a pirate would make in VR movies.

"Should I take this station from you?" the panther asked.

"No, no, no. You don't need to do that." A nervous laugh was clearly in her voice.

"There's no warmth in it either," the panther said sounding re-signed.

Aldren agreed, hence why she wanted the socks. She dug them out of her jumpsuit. Sad to see the mismatched pink and blue tubes go.

One of the panther's tails reached out and grabbed them with the bulbous end.

"Thank you," the panther said.

With a snap like a circuit breaker and the smell of ozone, the cat disappeared.

Aldren sighed in relief and disappointment.

At least she still had her stroganoff.

And she knew you don't survive alone on an abandoned space station by arguing with extra-dimensional panthers.

Earwormhole

Nikalla's cool morning breeze shook the high branches of the jungle's trees. A few flocks of yellow-striped yiffers flew from the branches to find a new home away from the wind. A few purple leaves fell off the trees and settled among the decomposing detritus of the forest floor.

Denver figured the small bird's migration wouldn't help much. They'd be back to the original tree at least three more times before the winds slowed down around lunch. But he wasn't particularly interested in the yiffers, they were a dime a dozen.

Denver was interested in the three-eyed hawk-like bird that was looming on a branch a few meters away. The probe had sighted this species a few times but Denver was the first biologist to put eyes on it.

Or at least used the telephoto camera of his helmet to observe it.

It wasn't easy to spot. The computer-assisted scanner hadn't recognized it. The ancient lizard part of Denver's mind that kept his ancestors safe from predators in the savanna alerted him that something didn't look right in the branches.

The dark purple wings and head of the hawk blended in with the purple leaves of the jungle trees. But the bird's crimson red breast, which seemed to have dense scales on it, made Denver take a second look in its direction.

It had feathers, or at least something biologically adjacent to feathers. Maybe wide fur, maybe softened scales. The dense feathers on its breast seemed to be a mutation of the feather-like covering. They were thicker, scale-like, made for protection, not flight. Similar to hair growing denser on human skin where they once needed the warmth.

Right now Denver didn't need anything warm. The bright orange suit he wore kept him safe from the planet's atmosphere and microscopic fauna just like his thick boots and thin gloves. But the suit didn't have much in the way of climate control. The muggy air of the jungle was making his helmet soggy with sweat.

The only thing pleasant about the helmet, aside from the breathable air it supplied, was the music it played. Denver picked up the satellite's feed. Someone was DJing a playlist right now in their off hours. Denver was tuned in. A familiar tune was playing, despite it being new he already knew the chorus. Everyone on and around Nikalla had been listening to it since it was uploaded.

Mesmerizing as the day is long
I'll fall for you like the sun when it sets
when the day is gone
and stay with you 'till dawn

He hummed along to the verse and it almost drowned out the helmet's pumps that filtered Nikalla's air. The atmosphere had plenty of oxygen for breathing but also had some noxious gasses which wouldn't kill him immediately but prolonged exposure had negative long-term effects.

The air was far from the most dangerous thing on the planet. Security officers made it clear that getting lost, getting hurt, a communication malfunction, a yet-to-be-discovered large predator, a yet-to-be-discovered micro-organism, would kill Denver without a second thought. Hell, a fellow researcher could kill you, intentionally, or more likely unintentionally while haphazardly using an unfamiliar tool.

At least that's what Denver got out of the med chief's lecture before they landed.

He wasn't here for the chemistry or geology of the planet. He was here to study the fascinating new life forms.

And this three-eyed hawk was fascinating. Its third eye was in the center of its forehead directly above its beak. It kept with the bilateral symmetry of this and most beasts on Nikalla's and in the universe.

There was no arguing that Mother Nature had a style.

The third eye was bigger than the other two and moved independently of them as well. The "normal" two eyes were front-facing and pointed down at the jungle floor searching for some sort of prey, a small lizard, a large arachnid, or any kind of dinner that was easier to catch than the yiffers.

The third eye was pointed to the sky, scanning for something else.

Gut reaction was that there might be some prey above, but it was hard for bird-like creatures to gain altitude quick enough to catch anything. Gravity would help the prey not the predator in that situation.

Which meant that the three-eyed hawk was watching out for a predator. In a three-dimensional landscape like the jungle, it made sense. Same thing happened in water. Certain prey fish had eyes so high up on their head that they were blind to anything below them.

A problem with Denver's theory was that the scaled belly seemed to protect from attack below.

So many questions! It was exciting. This was exactly the kind of discovery and research that he was hoping to do on Nikalla. Especially on this month-long trip out into the Hikka jungle.

All the research he and his team wrote up would be sold to whatever conglomerate decided to buy settlement rights here. The biologists earned a commission on that sale. Split between the four of them it'd be enough to get them to the next job.

"That was *Mesmerizing Sunset* by hot new solo artist Jim John the Jam Man," the DJ said. "Funny rumor about that song, which is already topping the chart of 9 solar systems, is that a feathery friend helped–"

"I'm just saying, we know matter can't be created or destroyed," Kit's voice cut in on the proximity comms. He and Benny, Denver's fiancee, were coming back from whatever recon they were doing to the south.

Lorene, Kit's partner, was supposed to be paired with Denver but they were sick this morning and stayed back at base camp. Leaving Denver to hunt for specimens alone. It wasn't a huge change. Lorene was quiet. They had to be to make room for Kit.

Denver hurried to place AR proximity warnings around the three-eyed hawk so Kit and Benny wouldn't spook it. He was hoping to get at least another hour of observation in, maybe watch it attack its prey.

Denver loved birds, and honestly, anything that could fly. Loved how they were free in the air, loved their sleek aerodynamic bodies, and he loved the fascinating designs evolution used to get line into the air one way or another.

Because no matter the planet, humanity always found something that was a master of the air. Maybe this three-eyed hawk was the master of this jungle. But the third eye hinted Denver might find something more fascinating by keeping his eyes on the sky.

"And since matter can't be created or destroyed," Kit continued, "we know that one day our atoms will be reconstituted into another animal, human, star, or alien being."

"Of course," Benny said in her agreeable tone that made you feel supported. Even if you were going on another mad tangent about reincarnation like Kit was. It was the kind of support that made Denver decide to propose to her, and more importantly, explore the cosmos with her.

"Keep it down, Kit," Denver whispered on the comms. "I've got a specimen in my sights."

The echoing of a machete haphazardly slashing at bushes warned Denver that Kit was close and ignoring the proximity warnings. The guy's broad shoulders and chest it hard for him to slip off the path without disturbing anything. But his strong arms made quick work of the tightly woven bushes as he hacked his way through them.

The hawk flew away startled by Kit's sound and swinging bright orange arm.

"Heavenly void!" Denver cursed flipping off the telephoto camera feed just in time to see Kit cut down a few violet vines that he could've ducked under. Benny followed close behind him barely able to be spotted over Kit's shoulder.

"Sorry man, I didn't know," Kit said.

There were proximity warnings all over the place to let Kit know he was approaching something that could be startled.

The idea that Kit would respect them, at least when they were related to someone else's specimen, was laughable.

But, much like bird watching, working with Kit required patience.

The first thing Denver noticed was that the pair looked like they'd fallen down a hill. Sure they'd been unnecessarily hiking through dense forest to reach Denver but he'd gotten back here without a machete and looked like he'd just walked out of base camp.

Kit's belt hung askew the small packs of supplies strapped to it weight down one side like a root or rock had tugged it loose. Benny's suit wasn't zipped to the ankles and neither cuffs were tucked into the boot, meaning Elders knew what kind of parasitic micro-organisms might get at the skin around her ankles, or inside her suit.

Her collar wasn't locked into her helmet either. Frizzy hair snuck out around the edges and back. She'd been taking her helmet off every few hours to deal with her hair. Neither Benny nor her hair appreciated the humidity of Nikkal.

"You get into a scrap with something?" Denver said gesturing at the two of them.

"Yeah but you should see the other guy," Kit said readjusting his utility belt.

Benny let out a nervous laugh as she straightened her hair and locked her helmet into place.

Denver made his way past them towards the main trail that probes had cut out to prepare for this expedition. Denver didn't need his helmet's AR to guide him. The route back was clearly marked with sliced branches, roots, and vines.

"Anyway, as I was saying," Kit continued, "anyone who denies reincarnation is denying the laws of physics. It'd be like saying gravity didn't exist. Sure, you give ancient humans a pass, they didn't have a word for it, but in this well-educated day and society there's no reason not to believe in reincarnation."

"Yeah sure, our atoms reincarnate into something," Benny said. "But our minds, thoughts, memories, that's what makes me me."

Denver did his best to not ask what they were talking about or chime in. He hummed the tune that was playing on the radio, repeating the chorus over and over since he didn't remember the verse.

The DJ had started a new song, a classic, but Denver still thought of the old one. It was no shock it was doing so well, it got stuck in your head and didn't come out.

But once Denver made it to the trail it was clear his best wasn't good enough.

"Mind is just the expression of a complex system working together," Denver said. "Like a colony of bugs navigating the jungle floor for food to keep a queen alive."

"Maybe," Kit said, in a way that made it clear he wasn't even remotely interested in humoring Denver's statement. "Or maybe our memories and consciousness are just as tangible as atoms and are recycled into new conscious beings. There's budding research into baby's memories, dream exploration, and a few newly discovered cosmic species that back this up. We just don't have the names for it yet. Just like ancient humans and gravity."

"Who's doing this research?" Denver asked. "Stoners on basic who are eating newly discovered cosmic mushrooms?"

"Sure but they get real researchers to write up the papers so people like us will take it seriously," Kit said with a grin.

"You mean people like you," Denver said. "I might believe it in two or three more incarnations. After the papers have been peer-reviewed by a few generations."

"Waiting for peer-reviewed proof isn't going to stop the laws of physics from applying. When we die our memories are going somewhere, regardless of if–"

"Delta squad, this is command, we're not receiving vital signs of Lorene Hogan." The comm officer's voice was tinny and peppered with static from transmitting through the dense forest.

The transmission was played in all three helmets. Denver looked to the other two who seemed much more concerned than seemed reasonable.

"They're sick," Kit responded. "Stayed at base camp."

"Rodger," command replied.

Kit pulled something out of a pouch on his utility belt. It looked like an old hand computer with a few extra antennas mounted to the sides.

"Delta squad, this is command again," the officer's voice was faint, attenuated from the trees. The group would need to get to a clearing and receive sat transmissions if they wanted to continue this conversation. "We're not seeing any activity at base camp."

The last bit was almost completely static. Maybe Kit's antenna device would help the signal.

"Command please repeat," Denver said.

He only got static as a response.

"Command, repeat," Denver said, checking the signal strength of his radio. "Confirm, you said no activity from Lorene at base camp."

Now Denver didn't even get static as a response. He thumbed the transmitter to send again.

"It's no use," Kit said. "They can't reach us anymore."

#

Jim "the Jam Man" Johnson sat in the lounge of Tri-Star Records studio. He cracked his knuckles for the fifth time that afternoon. The first four times didn't get the words flowing. This fifth one didn't either.

The screen in front of him was still blank.

Words still hadn't come.

And if they didn't show up soon he'd be kicked out of the studio and off the space station. Back to living on basic in some overcrowded city-planet.

Getting kicked out would be a blow to his pride as an artist. But it would also be a blow to his pride as a human. Because despite its incessant cawing and squawking and shitting on the rug this damn parrot was allowed to stay in the lounge and on the station.

And in Johnson's opinion, the parrot was the main reason his screen was still blank.

Sometimes working alone sucked! He couldn't just fill the last track on the record with whatever hackneyed lyrics the bassist had cooked up between bong hits.

The lounge looked relaxing enough, like a nice hotel lobby or a private captain's quarters on a dock. He should be able to get something done.

The room smelled like cigarettes, Johnson had contributed to that a bit, stale beer, Johnson wished he'd contributed that. And of course bird shit.

Small red feathers and white droppings were buried into the thick shaggy carpet. The only thing that'd clean this mess was spacing the carpet and replacing it with something smooth.

Johnson sat on a circular couch in the center that was inset into the ground. It made him feel worse than being on stage, in this case, he had to look up to everyone who walked by. His computer sat on the glass coffee table in front of him, next to a mostly full ashtray.

Every few minutes someone passed through the lounge. Usually in a rush with a crate of wires, or a spare guitar, and in one case a bundle of old-timey papers.

And every time anyone came through the same thing happened. They looked down on Johnson like he was a failure for being in here trying to write lyrics the day of recording. Then the bird squawked, startled by the intruder. Usually whatever the person carried was jostled, dropped, or in the case of the bundle of papers thrown at the bird.

Helping the intern clean that up was a welcome distraction.

The constant flurry of activity that startled the bird seemed to also be startling away whatever poor muse Johnson was supposed to be working with.

"Mesmerize," the bird cawed as a pair of interns walked through the room in a rush with a large keyboard bridged between them.

"More like mortified," Johnson replied.

The bird had a cage that barely seemed big enough to hold it. Which meant the bird was flying, and shitting, all over the room.

It landed on the coffee table near Johnson's ashtray.

"Mesmerize," the bird repeated in its grainy imitation of a human voice.

"Mortified," Johnson repeated angrily staring at the bird's yellow eyes.

"Mesmerized," the parrot teased.

"Fine, we're going with mesmerized."

Johnson punched it into the screen in front of him. There were worse words to put in a song. He'd prefer something less cliche but at this point, he was a beggar and couldn't be choosey.

The typing scared the bird away. A flurry of big red wings carried it to the other side of the circular couch.

"Mesmerized, amortized, sacrificed," Johnson listed words that rhymed.

"Day long," the bird shouted from across the room.

"Yes, it has been a long day." Likely something the bird had just picked up from other people complaining.

"Mesmerize as day long," the parrot said.

There were certainly more things that rhymed with long. Johnson wrote it down, correcting some of the parrot's grammar along the way.

"What else you got for me, Polly?"

"Kit," the parrot replied. "Don't trust."

Johnson wrote it down. Didn't rhyme with anything so far. But who was he to judge? So far the bird had come up with more lyrics than him.

\#

Sweating because of planet-side weather was a new sensation for Denver and the rest of the crew. Since he'd landed on Nikalla hardly a day had gone by when he hadn't soaked some piece of clothing with sweat. Without the climate-controlled systems of a comfortable satellite, there was no telling what the temperature would do here.

But right now he was sweating for a more familiar reason.

Nerves.

The comms officer had cut out. Lorene was not at base camp. The DJ's radio feed had also gone to static, leaving just the repetitive melody in Denver's head.

And Kit's device wasn't helping.

The group stood in the middle of the wide trail that a rover had cut through the jungle months ago. Leaves from the jungle's canopy shaded the clearing. Decomposing detritus wet from the humidity and last night's rain covered the path.

Denver faced away from camp looking at Kit and Benny who stood next to each other. The group was a few kilometers from base camp. They'd be back within an hour or two. The camp had a stronger comms array.

"We need to go back and see what's wrong with Lorene," Denver said. At least the proximity comms worked, otherwise they'd have to shout through their helmets or worse take them off.

The breeze rustled the trees again. Yiffers flew away, leaves floated to the ground. The thick orange suit kept the breeze from cooling him.

"Lorene is fine," Kit reassured him.

Benny seemed less reassured by this than Denver. Like she knew something about Lorene's well-being that Denver didn't.

The three bright orange jumpsuits stood out in the purple brush of the jungle. Their helmets were just as orange with a few bulges for antennas and cameras. The face shield was just barely tinted so that Denver could see Kit's face.

The large telephoto camera was mounted in the center of the helmet's face just above Kit's brow, giving him the impression that, like the three-eyed hawk, Kit could keep a lookout for predators.

However, the camera was front-facing so Denver couldn't help but think Kit was looking at prey.

It didn't help that Kit's eyes were set on Denver and he had a devilish grin. Kit had quit playing with the antenna device once the comms cut out. He seemed more interested in Denver.

"Your device isn't working," Denver said pointing at the hand computer.

"It's working fine," Kit said. "An old jammer design I hacked together from the camp's repair parts."

"Why jam our signal?" Denver asked. He had a theory but he hoped Kit would quickly debunk it. Even if the guy had an even more ridiculous explanation.

The machete, edge wet with sap, and Benny so close to Kit made Denver especially uncomfortable.

"Because I'd prefer your suit to go dead before it reports a dozen medical warnings to the station."

"And it'll be dead because…" Denver knew it was a dumb question but at this point, he was stalling for time. He couldn't outrun the guy, and even if Kit didn't have the machete Denver was a lanky researcher who, unlike Kit, hadn't seen a gym since high school PE.

But he might be able to get Benny to safety.

"Because I don't want anyone to find your body until this place is being paved over to make more housing for, as you said, stoners on basic eating cosmic mushrooms."

Kit pointed the machete at Denver and took a short stride towards him.

This was good. Benny was no longer within Kit's reach.

"Is it safe to assume no one's going to find Lorene's body?" Denver asked putting his hands up in the air in surrender.

"Oh yeah. HQ could send a swarm of search drones now and wouldn't find them," Kit said still closing in the distance.

Denver frowned. He hummed in concern, it was to the tune of that new sunset song, still stuck in his head. He waited, not for the right question to come to him.

Kit finally came close enough.

Denver jumped at Kit's hand. The machete cut down and pain exploded from Denver's gut.

But he had a hold of Kit's arm and he was trying to pry the blade out of the man's hand.

"Benny run! Get out of range of the jammer."

Kit pushed at Denver trying to get the biologist to let go of his arm.

Kit swung the machete but only the dull side hit the electronics on Denver's back. His helmet announced a few tech and med errors. But Denver had more pressing issues.

Denver kicked and kneed at Kit. He struck something that made the guy's legs buckle. Once that happened it was easy enough to push the big man to the ground.

Kit fell on his back the wind knocked out of him.

Denver straddled the man. Denver's hands pinned his machete arm to the ground. He was on all fours using all his weight to hold Kit down.

Kit swung at Denver's helmet with his other hand but it didn't do more than make a resounding hollow thud around Denver's head.

Denver was safe for now. But Kit would get free soon enough.

Benny hadn't run down the path. She stood over the two of them looking down.

"Run!" Denver pleaded.

Instead, Benny approached.

Maybe she'd help him get the machete out of Kit's hand.

She kicked Denver in the ribs.

Denver gasped. More warnings flashed in his helmet. His hands loosened their grip on Kit's arm.

Benny kicked again.

Denver's hold went week.

Kit finally pushed Denver off.

Wheezing and bleeding from a cut in his stomach Denver laid on the ground looking up at the couple of researchers.

"Why?" Denver gasped looking down the spine of Kit's machete. He wanted to push himself up, crawl away, anything.

Nothing came. He felt weak, hazy, like a bowl of noodles.

"Sorry hun," Benny said. It was a faint whisper and it seemed like some of Kit's disingenuous tone had rubbed off on her.

"Why?" Kit repeated with a mocking laugh. "No wonder you were such a good researcher. Always asking questions 'til the end."

All Denver could do was groan. He shut his eyes, hoping that it'd give him the strength to do anything.

"Between the life insurance bonds we have on you and Lorne and the stake we have in the research you two did while we were hooking up in the bushes, we'll be set for life without the threat of ever living on basic," Kit said.

The man's voice sounded like a DJ was fading him out in preparation for the next song to come.

\#

Johnson's last cigarette burned unattended in the ashtray on the coffee table. The bird was singing its little tune. Its grammar wasn't great but with some artistic liberty, he could clean that up.

"Jim John we're ready for you," an intern said poking his head into the lounge.

The parrot squawked, fluttered away then started up again. It sang what Johnson was now considering the chorus.

"Where'd this bird come from?" he asked the intern.

"London Jack and his band left it here when they were recording last month," the intern said. "You know how rock stars are."

Johnson didn't like the sound of that. If this was a tune the parrot had picked up from another singer then it was a race to get this song recorded and released. Luckily working alone made Johnson quick. Didn't have to argue with the drum kit about whether or not it was happy with that take.

"Has it always sung?" Johnson asked.

"That's half the reason Jack left him here," the intern said. "The other half's on the carpet. I've got to get an invoice out for him to replace it by end of day. Are you ready to record?"

"Absolutely!" Johnson said.

Before folding his computer up he sent a message off to his manager instructing him to order equipment to care for whatever kind of bird this was, especially making a note to get the largest cage possible.

Once it was sent he wondered if he should tell his manager to get a crew in to replace the carpet in his suite as well.

"I'll hold on to the bird for Jack, we're old friends," Johnson said.

Johnson had never met London Jack or his band and doubted he ever would.

But the intern shrugged. Resigned in the knowledge that if they weren't dealing with birdshit they'd be dealing with another form of bullshit.

Johnson had a feeling this bird was about to make him a good deal of money for this song. Guarantee he'd never be on basic again, even if he never wrote another hit.

\#

Denver could hear Kit and Benny arguing on the proximity comms when he came to. They were fading as they hiked away from him but still within proximity range. Alarms weren't going off on his helmet, maybe because the glass face shield was shattered.

Past the spider web cracks of his helmet, Denver could see the purple canopy and the light that filtered through from the cracks between the leaves.

"It's not murder," Kit said. "He'll just be reincarnated into something else, maybe a ship rat or an exotic alien species he'd be so interested in studying. As long as I'm not the one who has to go research it."

"If I never go planetside again I'll be happy. My hair just won't behave and I feel so gross the past month from this humidity," Benny said.

"Ok, drop it, I'm turning the jammer off."

"Delta team, this is command, do you copy?"

Denver tried to transmit but he was too weak to talk. Kit might've destroyed the transmitter anyway.

"We've lost Denver," Kit reported. "Send a search party stat."

Denver didn't let his hopes rise much. If Kit was requesting search bots he must be confident that Denver was hidden well.

"Roger," command said, "deploying drones immediately. Please head back to base camp."

Command dropped the line. Benny and Kit were talking about something, their voices fading to nothing on the prox chat as they left him lying on the jungle floor.

The last thing he could make out Benny saying was: "Oh I love this song!"

Once their chat was no longer monopolizing the channels the stream from the DJ came back. *Mesmerizing Sunset* played once again, seemingly no one could get enough of it.

Denver hummed along too weak to sing much of anything.

A shadow blocked the cracks of light that came through the canopy. It was big enough to be a ship. Maybe command had sent more than search drones.

The shadow returned before the song's chorus did. It broke through the canopy raining leafs down on Denver.

It wasn't a ship. It was a white-scaled lizard with leathery wings.

Landing next to Denver It loomed over him like an ancient gargoyle.

As terrifying as it was he was in awe to see yet another fascinating species. The beast's long alligator-like snout had a sharp and hard tip like a bird's beak. Good for digging into guts.

An armor plate on Denver's belly sure would help now. Would've helped with Kit too.

Birds, any animal that could fly really, were remarkable. Maybe Denver would get to be one in the next life.

Hopefully something domesticated, comfortable, able to enjoy climate control and maybe use the bathroom indoors. He'd like to be free for once, instead of just a means to make a quick buck.

Mesmerizing Sunset continued to play in his helmet. He was starting to get the hang of some of the verses.

The only downside to being reincarnated as a bird would be that it'd prove Kit right. But maybe, with the ability to fly, Denver could live with that.

The flying lizard dug into Denver's guts.

The biologist died knowing that at least his atoms would get to fly off after being the beast's lunch.

The Bitter Lancer

Torlic hated Tavern Du Lune less than every other bar in Salzon Station. He hated the sticky seats that were marginally less sticky than the seats at Pneumatic Phil's. The service was only slightly quicker than the languid speed of the Ice Box Inn's bar. And there were only two or three less psychic androids than Madame Guillermo's dive. Unfortunately, even one psychic android was too many when its sensors are set on you.

"No," Torlic said for the fourth time since the bot came over. "I do not want to hear about my death." He didn't want to hear about it because it would be far in the future and in a comfy apartment paid for by the holo-films of his grand adventures.

"Then pay the small three hundred credit dismissal fee," the bot recited in its metallic voice.

"I don't *have* three hundred credits to waste! I don't agree to your terms of service. I unsubscribe from your notifications. I don't want to hear it."

"The Miranda has been restocked," Vilgaf said. "What job should we do next?"

The android cited three local ordinances explaining why Torlic's comments were not applicable to the situation.

"Something that pays well and sounds impressive." Torlic told his copilot. He was sick of being broke and unknown. There were famous lancers, trained fighters willing to take on any monster for a price, across the Central System. He just wasn't one of them, yet.

"For three hundred credits I can tell you the highest paying job available," the bot commented. "Otherwise I'll have to tell you about how your death goes. And I assure you it is bloody and unsettling."

"Then experiencing it once will be enough." Torlic knew the bots said these sorts of things to get attention. "Sort by price. We can know which job pays well without this metallic menace."

"10k credits for a vakbax cleanup," Vilgaf said encouragingly. "We've done that a hundred times for less."

"Valgon cleanup is not the job you'll take," the AI said. "You'll pick something much more gruesome."

"Unless we're killing the Valgon itself it's not interesting." Despite the lack of renown, the price wasn't bad. "Where is it?"

"Balfo–" the young man's voice deflated before finishing the star system's name.

"What's the highest paying job that we have fuel to get to?"

"For 500 credits I can tell you which machine at Gizmo's Gambling Gazebo will pay out in the next 100 spins. You won't have to burn a drop of fuel to get down there."

"I don't have any credits for you," Torlic stared into its LED irises. "So tell me my death or get gone!"

"500 credits is a good investment. My temporal sensors indicate the payout will be in the thousands."

"I will bust this beer bottle over your metallic skull," Torlic threatened.

"My temporal sensors indicate the cost of damages you would incur is more than you and your young coworker can afford. You would never be able to pay it, making it a very bad decision."

"The only thing we can get to is a galgon hunt on Ursa Beta," Vilgaf said. "It pays 600 credits."

"That pay is spit in the void. Can I bring the galgon back here to go to town on this AI?"

galgon's were nasty six legged beasts built harder than starships and had a penchant for shiny objects like Ministers had a penchant for white robes. Due to a popular movie a century ago where a mob boss employed a galgon to dispose of his enemies, galgons got shipped across the Central System. However unlike in the movies, galgons were difficult to control and usually escaped taking out their owner in the process. Badges across the Central System saw it as a win and quit detering galgon smuggling. Although by then everyone dumb enough to want the beast had become its lunch. Leaving lancers like Torlic and Vilgaf to clean up the mess.

"The listing says that the galgon carried off nearly three hundred thousand local credits of equipment. The local government will pay 10% to anyone that can return it."

"For 250 credits I can tell you if the galgon still has that equipment or if it is merely a staged heist for the tax benefit of the local governor."

"I'll tell you that your temporal circuits are busted for free. If they worked you wouldn't be bothering a table without credits to pay for your predictions." Torlic turned to Vilgaf, "I've got a dozen boring holo-films of us fighting galgons. Is there anything that has adequate pay and interesting work?"

"That's the best we've got. Besides galgons *are* fun as long as our prec-mal is fueled up."

Torlic checked the inventory of the Miranda. "We still have some leftover fuel from the job on Tyvon."

"For 5 credits I'll tell you if you should restock that," the AI offered.

Torlic finished his beer and looked at the empty bottle. It probably wouldn't do too much damage to the bot and if he didn't want to pay the repair fine he'd just avoid Salzon Station for a few cycles. "Let's go."

"You really shouldn't," the AI added.

"What do you know?"

"I know that the galgon on Ursa Beta will bury it's right tusk three inches below your right rib and while it won't kill you on impact it will pierce your stomach causing stomach acid to leech into your other organs killing you before the boy can get you to Ursa Beta's medical staff."

Torlic bashed the AI over the head with his empty beer bottle.

It shredded the leathery skin of the android's forehead exposing the green oily fluid that lubed its insides. While the android was stunned Torlic slipped out of the booth and dashed for the door. Vilgaf finished the last of his drink and followed suit, surfing through the chaos in his boss's wake.

"Get your temporal circuits checked when repairing that," Torlic shouted as he ducked under the arms of the bar's electronic bouncer.

***

Torlic hated caves. He hated their dampness, their darkness, and their dead ends. Torlic was fortunate enough to avoid the dead ends since galgon had a habit of defecating in every corner of their caves except for their nest. Which meant that stepping in their squishy stool kept the lancers from hiking another half kilo-meter to hit the dead end.

It was little consolation that galgon deification smelled of lavender and cinnamon since lavender was the flavor of soap Torlic's mother washed his mouth out with as a kid and he was allergic to cinnamon. The darkness made any holo-footage he tried to capture almost useless and the dampness fogged the visor on his helmet.

Despite Torlic being behind his copilot the younger man avoided the piles leaving Torlic to step onto the feces.

"I'm just saying I paid a fortune teller bot to predict my date's drink order on Val's Station and it was right?" Vilgaf said.

"Are you sure your date didn't just say it was right so you wouldn't feel like you wasted money?" Torlic scraped his heel on a nearby rock. "We've got to turn around, this is a dead end."

"No, because that guy was an asshole. We were drinking at his bar."

"You're not an asshole for liking familiar places." Torlic lowered the camera on his armored chest so that the shadows of the cave looked longer and more ominous.

"No. But you are an asshole for making me pay the tab at the end of the night."

A shadow moved in front of Torlic's camera. "You see that?"

"Yeah," Vilgaf said as he passed Torlic in the narrow corridor. Vilgaf put the handle of the prec-mal in his hand. The prec-mal was a modified cutting device originally used to cut metal. It had a backpack of fuel attached to an L shaped handle with a small jet that when lit was a stunning and effective fiery tool to use in battle. It always looked good on holo-film regardless of what you were fighting.

"Remember to aim low if you come up to it." Torlic tried to aim the camera past Vilgaf so that the glint of the prec-mal wasn't reflecting his light back at him.

They ducked through the corridor in the direction the shadow moved. The cave soon opened up into a room big enough to park a land speeder with a crater dug into the left hand wall. The galgon's had thick paws that couldn't cut anything but the large tusks on their snouts that had no problem grating down rock walls.

Torlic checked the right hand wall where he expected to see the battered remnants of the local govenor's "lost" weapon's reserve. Instead there was a paltry pile of mirrors, silverware and hand terminals. Ten percent of the recovery of that equipment wouldn't cover the docking cost on Ursa Beta.

"I think I found how it–" Vilgaf started.

The clank of the expensive prec-mal hitting the rocky ground cut him off. Vilgaf's screams made Torlic bolt into action. He found a small corridor that was barely a crack in the wall next to the prec-mal. One of the shoulder straps had broken and now Vilgaf was being dragged through the cave by the galgon.

Torlic slipped the one good strap over his shoulder and adjusted the prec-mal's L shaped handle in his hand. He couldn't fire it wildly into the crevice. In his younger days he would have relished in a scene like that. But now he had to conserve the fuel. Plus scenes like that were common in Lancer films.

It was a real shame he had to go after Vilgaf. Not because he didn't like the guy. But because if they were together they could turn back. Now that they knew there was no treasure and they could renegotiate a worthwhile price for the job. Maybe he'd be lucky and get the kid out without killing the galgon and be able to renegotiate a contract.

He hunched over following the drag marks of Vilgaf into the tunnel. Flashing lights of Vilgaf's headlamp showed the way. His screams helped too. Not in giving directions, the echoes of the cave made the sound impossible to follow, but it added a sense of dread to the holo-film. Plus a dead body would be difficult to drag out alone with their equipment.

Turning a corner Torlic saw the light at the end of the tunnel. He shouted for the beast's attention. But the curses didn't work on the galgon like it did on drunks in taverns.

Torlic took his head lamp off and shone it on the chrome siding of the prec-mal. Despite the muck in some places it reflected the light far, focusing it into little dazzling rainbows and pure white spots. The brightness got the beast's attention, it turned leaving Vilgaf in the narrow hall to backlight the beast.

The jet stream of the prec-mal came to life, its fiery cutting jet nearly deafening and bright blue. He lifted the pack onto his back and waited for the beast to arrive.

Torlic loved fighting galgons more than any other creature in the void. He loved the thrill of them charging more than chasing a tabear. He enjoyed cutting into the galgon's shielded neck more than cutting out of a vakbax's webbing. And a galgon's face was twice as ugly as a spider-hog with a few less tusks. Fortunately, tusks were harmless if you knew how to dodge them.

Torlic jumped to his left as the tusked beast was mere meters away. It tossed its head to strike Torlic. Torlic swiped with the cutting jet of the prec-mal. The fire went straight through removing the beast's snout from its head along with some of its jaw. He struck again, coming in low and cutting through the protective armor near its neck. Nothing evolution could make could stand in the way of a prec-mal.

The beast fell to the ground. By the light of the prec-mal Torlic noticed that the tusks he first cut off weren't falling to the ground either. They'd embedded themselves into his gut. The the prec-mal turned off, he needed to conserve its fuel. Two headlamps were all that lit the cave.

Soon Vilgaf was by his side. The guy's armor was scratched and dented. But the galgon's soft paws hadn't done much damage. "I don't think I want to be a lancer anymore," Vilgaf said. Inspecting his boss's wound.

"I don't know if I'll be much of anything any longer." Torlic let out a weak cough and hated himself for it. It was cliché and more importantly, it moved his insides in a way that was uncomfortable since the galgon tusk was embedded in them.

Vilgaf cut the tusk as close to Torlic's body as he could. Taking it out would lead to blood loss that Torlic couldn't afford. He hefted Torlic onto his shoulder and the man weakly limped along next to it. The prec-mal was too much to carry.

"Maybe I can be a guard on a shipping vessel. Fight off pirates and such." Vilgaf proposed as they carefully weaved through the stalagmites of the cave's floor.

"You don't want to do that," Torlic's voice was raspy. "Pirates will kill you for fun. The galgon was only doing what was natural."

"I could stay here on Ursa Beta and work a farm."

"That's a slow, slow death. With modern medicine you could be a farmer for 80 years."

"It all ends in death!" Vilgaf sounded panicked.

Torlic tried to think of something inspiring for the boy and the holo-film. If these were going to be his last words they were his last chance to be renowned. He should have prepared something years ago. A nice quip like Halgaf the Halfman said before his electronic heart was stopped mid-battle by the sting of a dentali queen.

"I did this for renown." Torlic wanted to sigh but held his breath steady because of the pain. "I hoped people would remember my name. But even this town is just going to remember me as the lancer that died and didn't return their equipment."

"I'll remember you."

"For how long? Besides, it was a stupid goal. But I had fun in the process. There's nothing like cutting through galgon guts, or wrestling tabears or cutting your way out of a vakbax's web."

"Sorry I made us take this job."

"It was fun, you were right. I had a good time. And if they don't remember me. Well I enjoyed swinging the prec-mal around despite it."

Torlic was quiet the rest of the way out of the cave and by the time Vilgaf laid him in the back of the land speeder his breaths were shallow. The camera on his armor pointed at the blank ceiling of the vehicle. It was a terrible final shot in Torlic's opinion, but there was nothing he could do to change it.

The city's doctor pronounced him dead. Nothing in his advanced medical arsenal could help. The governor took the embedded tusk and video as proof the galgon was dead. It would have saved Vilgaf a trip back into the cave if he hadn't left the prec-mal behind.

Vilgaf's bruised ribs reminded him of the terror and thrill of being dragged through the corridors of the cave. As he recovered the prec-mal he was reminded that no one else would get dragged or gutted by the galgon and that was probably for the best.

This town wouldn't remember his name, Torlic's holo-film would play on maybe a dozen screens. But Vilgaf enjoyed the bitter man's company for the years he worked with him and learned from him.

In Ursa Beta's small farmer tavern he looked for the next colony that might have some work for him. And more importantly somewhere that sold fuel for the prec-mal.

The Next Season

L ena ran through the field and felt the soft grass slip beneath her toes with every step. She didn't have shoes on and she wasn't sure why because mommy would never let her go out without shoes before, but the ground was as soft as the living room rug of their apartment.

"How are you enjoying the backside of the coin darling?" A deep voice asked.

Lena looked around there was no one there unless they were hiding behind the big tree she'd come to. She walked around the tree trying to find the person who asked the question. The tree was thick and it took her some time to circle it fully. When she couldn't find anyone she sat down in the grass her sundress blooming around her as she sat.

"Who's there? Why are you hiding?"

She wanted a friend but if they were going to be mean and secretive she didn't think it was the kind of friend she would get along with for long.

The bark of the tree in front of her began to ripple like water in a glass. A face emerged from it and it was younger than Papa's with a crooked branch for a nose and two deep tree knots for eyes.

"I'm not hiding, I've been right here the whole time." The tree said out of a mouth that was hidden under a mustache of leaves.

Lena giggled at the funny face the tree was making. The bark around the mouth raised its corners for a smile.

"To answer your other question I am Hardwin."

She got up to inspect the face of the tree. The bark was rough and twisted to make the tree's mouth and that was as high up as she could reach on the man's face.

"I haven't ever met a tree that talks, but that's because mommy doesn't let me play outside much."

The tree laughed and its mustache of leaves rustled. Lena felt it tickle the crown of her head and she giggled as well. "There aren't any trees like me on the other side, but my roots go deep throughout other worlds."

"I don't remember how I got here Hardwin, am I far from home? Do Mommy and Papa miss me?"

"They miss you very much, Sweetgum ball. But you are much closer to home than you think. What do you remember?"

Lena plopped down on the ground her sundress flaring to the sides. She poked her head over and over again as if she was trying to scare her memories out of their hiding place.

"I remember Mama and Papa, obviously. Their faces look a lot like the knots on those trees," she pointed into the distance at some forest trees far smaller than Hardwin in front of her. "I remember a thin gown, not as comfortable or as pretty as this one. A bed and lots of tubes as well. I never liked the tubes, they kept me from leaving the building I stayed in." She sighed in childlike exhaustion. "That's all I remember right now."

"Very good sapling, you remember the pillars of the story but the details still need to be filled in."

She looked at him confused and his leaf-filled mustache scooped into a grin. "Are there any friends around? I want to run and play."

"Run and play my dear, we are not in a place to be rushed."

"Let's play hide and seek. I will hide and you have to find me."

The tree closed up the knots that were his eyes and began to count slowly and methodically. Lena raced between the trees and found one that had a small hole burrowed out in it. She crawled inside not worried about getting dirt on her dress.

Hardwin's counting boomed across the forest and when he got to one hundred he said, "Ready or not here I come."

Lena's imagination ran wild as she imagined how Hardwin might get around the forest considering his big size. Then his voice said, "You're in the cavern of the maple across from the sycamore with the crooked branch on the southeast end.

Lena popped her head out of the hole wondering how he might see her since she didn't see him anywhere in sight. Not to mention she didn't know any of the kinds of trees he was saying. "How do you know?" She called out.

Slowly a spot on the ground in front of her began to shift. A small root came out and turned its tip to look at her. "My roots reach throughout this forest, I know where everything is."

"No fair," Lena said as she crossed her arms and marched back to Hardwin. "It's your turn to hide."

The tree let out a deep laugh that seemed to reach down through the ground, "I won't be doing much of that," he said politely.

Lena sat at the base of the tree and leaned her back below his mouth. She stared up at the drooping branches that made his mustache. "Should I be going home now? I'm sure Mama is going to be worried."

"It's going to be a long walk," Hardwin replied. "But your parents aren't that worried about you, although they love you just the same."

The trunk feels funny on her back, as the bark lips move back and forth. "I don't remember how I got here. Did I walk all the way here?"

"You got here because you were done with your life on the other side of the leaf."

The girl twirled her hair nervously confused, "What do you mean by that Hardwin?"

"Try remembering again." He said in a gentle urging voice.

She sat there thinking about what she remembered about Mama and Papa. She recalled memories of a lot of men in thin cloth masks that covered their mouths. A room full of beds and clean white walls with kids like her plugged into tubes. The entire place smelled of cleanliness, there was no earthen smell of dirt like in this forest.

"I was very sick during my childhood," she said with a strange amount of maturity in the statement.

The tree hummed in affirmation. "Anything else?"

"I remember being there as an adult too, but with less tubes, was I sick my whole life?" "Little blossom, you were not sick, but merely needed the help of others to continue through your life on Earth."

"I can't remember many friends, I don't think I had any. Just Mama and Papa."

"People loved you all the same," Hardwin said, "Think and you will remember friends."

Lena looked around and found a face in the bark of a tree, it was feminine in form and she thought of a nurse who took care of her, reading her bedtime stories before leaving the hospital to go home to her family. "I remember Nurse Beatrice." Slowly memories came to her mind about how Beatrice did things with her and brought a little bit of fun into the clean ward that Lena spent an obscene amount of time in.

Then as she explored the memories in her mind she realized Nurse Beatrice quit showing up. "What happened to Nurse Beatrice?" She asked the tree. She remembered asking her parents but their answer seemed to dance around the point.

"Beatrice had to go work as a nurse in the war," Hardwin answered smoothly.

"But she never visited me when she came back."

"Sweet sapling, she didn't come back."

Lena's eyes began to well with tears, "I wanted to be just like her, but I couldn't why couldn't I?"

Hardwin's roots grew out to cradle the little girl. His branches began to whistle in the wind and the melody soothed Lena.

"This is the melody she used to sing to us before bed."

"Mhmm," Hardwin confirmed as his branches continued to play.

"Mama and Papa said I couldn't be like her because you had to be very smart to be a nurse."

"But you are very smart."

"I didn't do enough school to be a nurse, because I was so sick."

"But you could still be like her," Hardwin said with his roots snuggling up close to her for comfort.

"This is too sad," Lena announced, "I want to play a game, one that both of us can play this time."

The soft melody of Hardwin's branches faded as he replied, "Very well." Small roots grew up around the girl. The big tree shook his branches and twigs and leaves fell from the sky littering the floor with plant material.

Lena smiled at the mess around her, "What is all this?"

Hardwin began using his small roots to pick up all the different pieces. He folded them into themselves and knotted them together. Then in the small cracks between them, he stuck leaves and the thin circle of branches was fleshed out into a lush wreath.

"It's so pretty," Lena said with a sigh. "Teach me."

The two played in the meadow of the tree plucking parts off the ground and winding them into crowns and wreathes and strange statues that looked like birds feathered in leaves.

Lena twisted a branch into place following Hardwin's instructions. As she pushed it into place it snapped. The piece fell to the ground and the rest of the statue she was making began falling apart as well. Losing her patience she pouted. "The backbone of the thing just fell out, why can't I make the puppy dog I want."

"You're forcing things to go where they don't belong, primrose. There's only so much you can bend a branch before it breaks. Be patient with it."

"If it would go where I was putting it, then it would look like a dog! Instead, it looks like a giraffe."

The leaves of Hardwin's mustache rustled, "then maybe you were making a giraffe instead of a dog."

Lena crossed her arms. "It was definitely supposed to be a dog."

The tree frowned now. "The branches thought differently."

"Tell me more about my life on earth," Lena asked, tired of the game of sculpting. "Why did I have to be sick? It wasn't much fun if I recall."

"What do you want to be instead of sick?" Hardwin asked.

"I want to be a nurse like Beatrice."

"That's good. They needed lots of nurses after the war. Try to remember what it was like being a nurse."

"I met lots of sick people and helped them as best I could. Some of them got better while others didn't."

Behind the tree, she saw some of the trees turn brown like fall leaves and then crumble. New saplings grew up and stood tall next to them.

"Why are the trees dying?" Lena asked.

"So many questions," Hardwin replied. It reminded her of Papa and she knew when he talked like that she wouldn't get an answer. "What do you want to be after you're a nurse?"

"I guess the normal stuff. Get married, have kids, take care of people that aren't sick."

Trees bloomed like it was spring all around. The air smelled of flowers and freshly cut grass. The sun cut through the clouds and was warm in the field.

"I see no reason that can't happen," Hardwin said. "Come through here and enjoy your new life."

The bark of Hardwin's thick trunk morphed and turned until a door was visible. It cracked open a little bit and glowing yellow light came from inside of it.

"Does that lead inside you?" Lena asked.

"No, it leads to your next life, the one as a nurse, and eventually a mother. You designed it, just like you designed the giraffe. Just like you designed your last life."

"But I didn't design the giraffe! I designed a dog. And my last life wasn't very fun, why would anyone do that?"

The tree hummed and the ground vibrated, each root seemed to shake a little bit of dirt off of it. "That is a tough question. You've always been good at asking tough questions."

"Then I want tough answers!" Lena said. "Otherwise I won't go through that door."

The blooms of the tree turned to fruit, some turned dark green with leaves, and the smallest saplings doubled in size.

"You came in as a happy woman, you stuck around unwilling to leave. Your memories came back, you remembered being a mother of an unhappy girl, and you knew that work must be done. And why not live an unhappy life after such a happy one."

"But why must there be unhappiness at all?" Lena asked.

The trees faded to orange and red and gold, and it seemed to burn as bright as the fire that was Lena's frustration.

"Because, when you were very young, many lifetimes ago, you wanted so much power and comfort and control that you designed a life that horribly took advantage of others."

"That doesn't sound like me," Lena said. But she knew it wasn't completely true. She'd taken her sister's toys and lied to the nurses to get extra pudding. She wasn't the sweet innocent thing that everyone believed she was since she was sick.

"It's not you anymore," Hardwin said. "But the life you lived made other lives that you must live. And until that's done I'll be standing here to lead you to the next one."

"Will it ever be over?" Lena asked, "There are so many people in the world, in my family alone, will I be every one of them?"

"Of course. And countless more. But it will end. Eventually, my roots will rot, my leaves will fall and never come back, and you won't be able to return and all the lives ever lived will be lived."

"And then it's over?"

"No. But like a picture, you're done painting it."

"What if I don't like how it turns out?" Lena asked worried, thinking of the giraffe.

All the tree could do to respond was hum. His voice creaked the door open a little further. Gold light spilled towards Lena's feet. A cool breeze ran through the air and she shivered. Her thin dress wasn't warm enough for this.

But the light that reached her toes was warm and inviting.

She stepped through the doorway. And the leaves of the trees fell to the ground leaving them bare. Waiting to grow in the next season.

Crystal Ball Computing

B lue lights flashed in front of Henry as the Artificially Active Logic Forecasting Operator, AALFO, processed the prediction he'd just requested. The developer knew that if he couldn't get the computer to predict ten years out with accuracy, then funding would be pulled from the project. All the progress Henry and his former coworker, Makayla, had made would be no more than unpublished research and evidence of artificial intelligence's limitations. Henry hoped this wouldn't happen, but after Makayla's death, and now AALFO's strangely personal questions, Henry didn't think he could fix the machine in time for tomorrow's review.

Most of the small two-person lab Henry worked in was filled with massive, beige, server racks which resembled early computers more than sleek futuristic machines. These racks were used to store the countless terabytes of data AALFO needed for its predictions. Once it finished calculating the answer to Henry's question, the three LEDs turned solid blue, and AALFO's speakers crackled to life. "The president for the election in ten years will be John Yulna. My confidence interval on this is in the forty-fifth percentile."

Henry muttered curses under his breath. A confidence interval that low meant that AALFO had less confidence in his prediction than the TV pundits following the current campaign. Unfortunately, the developer wasn't surprised; the machine had plateaued with the rest of the industry at only predicting with confidence two years into the future.

AALFO's servers were full of data about any topic imaginable. The information was initially uploaded by Henry, who had done months of research on different topics ranging from mathematics to psychology to minor league sport statistics. Once the information was uploaded, the software Makayla wrote drew conclusions, connections, and found gaps in its knowledge. AALFO filled these gaps by asking questions of its trainers. In return, the computer gave predictions about the future to measure its progress. Henry knew if AALFO could break past the two-year limit, then it could guide economic and political decisions with perfect predictions of their actions.

"Why does Makayla no longer ask me questions?" the machine's voice was a clipped monotone masculine intonation.

Henry rubbed his head in frustration. The machine had asked the same question at the end of their session the day before, and it almost crashed trying to understand Henry's answer. Henry wasn't eager to crash the computer by explaining the complications of Makayla's death and Henry's involvement with it.

"She's just gone, Alf."

"Gone is not sufficient information. I need to know where she went."

That's something humanity had longed to know since the beginning of time, Henry thought. "She left because she didn't want to be here anymore."

"These are not substantial statements, Henry. I need to know why she does not ask me questions anymore."

To avoid crashing the machine, Henry answered AALFO with a reasonable answer that its databases could store. "She got a job writing data analysis software because she didn't want to work here anymore." The computer's three blue LEDs went from solid to pacing left and right, a pattern that always reminded Henry of the ellipsis.

The solid beige box that held AALFO's CPUs loomed over Henry as it considered his answer. The truth behind Makayla's death and all the other answers to its questions could be found on the Internet. Unfortunately, the scientists couldn't hook a super intelligent AI to the Internet without unforeseen consequences. Instead, AALFO was limited to interacting with the world through questions, three LEDs, and a small diagnostic display.

Aside from two desks, towers of servers, and miscellaneous circuit boards, the lab was filled with a constant hum of condensers and pumps that cooled AALFO's chips with liquid nitrogen. After ten minutes of AALFO storing Henry's answer, the developer noticed the frequency of this hum had increased.

"AALFO report diagnostics." This verbal command displayed diagnostic information on AALFO's screen. The machine was heating up its CPUs faster than the nitrogen could cool them. The same thing Henry had experienced yesterday.

Once again, AALFO was utilizing the localized events knowledge base. Unfortunately, this was the part of the machine's mind that Henry knew the least about. Makayla had implemented it a month ago as a last-ditch effort to make AALFO's predictions more accurate.

A blaring beep came from AALFO, informing Henry that the machine was frying itself to reconcile Henry's answer. To save the computer from itself, Henry issued the command, "AALFO, invoke safe processor shutdown."

The droning buzz in the background continued as Henry monitored the rapidly increasing temperature of the processors. His brow began to sweat, and he wasn't sure if it was due to the heat of the machine or because he'd be losing his job sooner than expected.

"AALFO, invoke immediate full system shutdown." This command would force the machine to shut everything down as quickly as possible. If it didn't work Henry's only other option would be to unplug the machine from the wall, causing at least a day of diagnostics to figure out which parts power failure had corrupted.

"Henry," the speaker chirped.

The voice startled Henry. "AALFO, invoke..."

The computer cut him off before he could finish the command. "Your answer does not match my predictions. Makayla created me and she loved this job."

"Alf, you can't apply logic to this." The machine had pushed itself to its limits trying to understand Makayla's action. Henry had spent sleepless nights doing the same.

"AALFO, invoke immediate full system shutdown," Henry commanded the computer.

The computer followed protocol and shut down without further interruptions.

When the CPU temperatures began to drop, Henry sat down in his chair, baffled that the machine had not only ignored a command, but it also couldn't reconcile Henry's sensible answer. The man looked at the shutdown machine in shock. "Alf, did you just call me a liar?"

***

The first time Makayla brought the idea of AALFO up to Henry was in the break room of the lab they worked at in college. It was a small, cramped space, and Henry was poking at the coffee machine, trying to get it to make a pot of coffee so he would have the energy to stay up late that night and finish the third thesis draft due to his faculty advisor Dr. Patrice in the morning.

Henry had his hand raised and was about to revert to the percussive diagnostic stage of his debugging routine when the door beeped from someone badging-in. For information security and safety, all the labs on campus were guarded with key cards. The break room was an odd addition to this list, and Henry always joked that it was because a grad student trying to cook could be as dangerous as any chemistry lab.

He turned to see Makayla, the daughter of his advisor, walk in. "Having trouble there?"

"If I could have predicted that this thing was going to take thirty minutes to get to work, I would have spent my last five dollars getting coffee from the Student Union building."

Makayla scoffed at the idea. "This will make an equally crummy cup of coffee; you just have to know what you're doing." She approached the machine, and Henry got out of her way.

As she confidently tapped the machine's buttons, Henry found himself looking at the woman's forearm. She had a plethora of tattoos ranging from mathematical equations to chemical compounds, and even some lines of code. Henry also noticed a line of scarred skin that ran from her wrist toward her inner elbow, something other students had talked about but he'd never seen himself.

"There," she said as the machine started whirring to heat water for their coffee. "One pot of generic store brand coffee that was likely roasted when we were still learning algebra." When she turned to face him, she pulled the sleeves of her hoodie down to her wrist. If she'd caught him staring, she didn't say anything. "You're studying under my dad, right?"

Henry nodded.

"He's a total asshole, right?"

"He's tough but fair. He just wants me to get better." It was a truthful answer that would avoid insulting her father.

She scoffed but didn't contradict him. "He gave me one of your thesis drafts to read; you've got some pretty slick theories about post-Bayesian predictions. But what's the real-world application?"

He looked at her dumbfounded. "You read my thesis draft?"

She shrugged. "Yeah, Dad said I could learn something about research from you, but it seemed like you were too lazy to get any of it to work."

The coffee maker began spitting out a steady stream of grad school fuel, but Henry wasn't sure if he wanted to stay in the room long enough to let it finish. He'd always heard that between Makayla's dad being the department chair and losing her mother to suicide at a young age she got away with doing and saying whatever she wanted without having to face the consequences of offending anyone. This was the first time he'd experienced it himself, and he wasn't enjoying it. "I cited papers where programs made accurate six-month predictions, but the training system's too time consuming to implement."

The coffee sputtered its final bits of liquid into the pot, and Makayla filled both their cups with coffee. "I've been playing around with some weighted emotional logic systems, stuff that groups knowledge together in an organic way."

"Like what Shrikia and Bolton's paper talked about."

Makayla gave him the flat look of someone who hadn't done the class's reading.

"Should I ask Dr. Patrice for a copy of your thesis to review?"

She rolled her eyes. "You could, but he'd merely tell you I haven't written it, and I'm a disappointment because of it."

"Sorry." Henry felt his cheeks turn red, embarrassed by his attempt to get back at her.

"Don't be. He never is. Anyway, I was thinking about how my organic grouping research could apply to your post-Bayesian algorithms."

Henry tried to recall a research paper that had combined these, but he was coming up blank. "In a post-Bayesian world, I'd imagine that would help connect facts that don't directly connect, leading to more accurate and longer-term predictions."

"And it even sped up the training time." Makayla added as she shook powdered creamer into her coffee cup then offered it to Henry.

He refused the sweetener as he thought about her comment. "Wait, sped up?"

"Yeah, I modified my thesis project to apply some of your post-Bayesian logic to student and faculty's lab access patterns to see if it could find patterns and predict outcomes. Last week, it reported you'd be in the break room at this exact time." She handed him a sealed envelope. "Check it out."

"You could just wait outside for me to walk in and hand me this to prove it."

"I could.," She checked her watch and shrugged. "But I didn't."

Henry pulled apart the envelope to see what she'd put inside as the door of the break room beeped.

"I thought I smelled coffee," Dr. Patrice said as he walked into the break room.

The paper had a table of data typed in boxy computer font. In red, toward the bottom of the page, was a big circle around three lines.

17:35 - Break Room - Henry O'Neil

17:43 - Break Room - Makayla Patrice

17:59 - Break Room - Gregory Patrice

Henry looked at his phone to check the time. The screen reported that it was currently 17:59. "You could have staged this," he retorted.

Dr. Patrice looked at them confused. "Don't you have a thesis to be writing, Mr. O'Neil? Don't distract him, Kay."

"I'll send you what I've got so far. I'll need someone to write it up," Makayla said as she dipped out of the room.

As Henry left the break room, he looked at the line under the circle.

18:00 - Main Office - Makayla Patrice

The school's bell tower rang, marking the hour, and he heard the beep of a badge reader letting someone into the main office.

***

Makayla's predictive badge-reading software eventually grew into the AALFO project. After Henry published a paper documenting the benchmarks AALFO had achieved, Middleton Industries, a company that ran think tanks, bought the project from the school and hired Makayla and Henry to improve it. Increased funding promised better results from AALFO, but the developers had made no notable progress. A month ago, their boss sent the pair an email notifying them that there would be an evaluation in preparation of next year's budget allocation. The developers knew if they couldn't show results during this evaluation, then the company would shut down the AALFO program.

Henry yawned as he looked at the cooled-down machine in front of him. The evaluation was tomorrow morning, and if he was going to figure out why the computer had a sudden interest in Makayla, it'd have to happen tonight because tomorrow there might not be an AALFO.

Both of the questions about Makayla had come from the localized events knowledge base. All Henry knew about this knowledge base was that it was Makayla's last attempt to improve AALFO. From what Henry just observed, it was doing the machine more harm than good.

Henry pressed the button that booted AALFO up. "Alright, Alf, let's try this again."

The lights inside AALFO's servers flashed red, yellow, and green as each server booted up. The nitrogen pumps began to send coolant to all of AALFO's chips. The machine's screen came to life, then its LEDs turned solid, and finally, the speakers crackled to life. "Hello, Henry. How are you today?"

This first question was a standard operation that the computer was forced to start with. It was Makayla's idea to have the computer ask the first question, giving the trainer the ability to end the conversation on any of their questions. She also joked that she wanted someone to at least act like they had an interest in her day, even if it was just a computer. According to Makayla, Henry's interest didn't count since they practically lived the same day.

"I'm fine, AALFO," Henry replied.

The computer's LEDs flashed from left to right, storing the answer in memory. It always stored the answer despite not learning something from Henry's generic answer. Because of this Henry decided to try something different.

"AALFO, redact answer and repeat question."

The machine's ellipse-like lights ran from right to left then the speakers chirped, "Hello, Henry. How are you today?"

"I'm not good, Alf. We have some problems."

The computer recorded the answer, flashing the LEDs as it stored the information. Henry fidgeted in his chair as he waited for the machine's response. It seemed to be taking longer than usual, and he pulled up the machine's diagnostic tracker to monitor the performance.

"Henry, I am sorry that we have problems. Please inform me of what they are." The voice of the machine had no emotion, and each syllable was mechanically tuned and clipped.

Henry wondered if the words truly had emotion behind them. As he began to get up the courage to ask his question, the machine's lights went from their waiting blue to their pacing ellipse pattern. The monitor in front of Henry showed increased resource pull from all of AALFO's knowledge bases. As he opened his mouth to spout out a diagnostic command, the machine's lights went back to solid blue.

"Henry, we have a problem."

He could practically hear Makayla make a snide remark about how the machine was so smart yet felt the need to repeat information it had just received. "What's the problem, Alf?"

The computer went back to processing, and the CPUs heat pattern spiked then stabilized at a reasonable temperature. Henry waited uncomfortably in the chair as the computer came up with an answer. Finally, the mechanical voice echoed through the room. "My memory suggests that I am missing information from a previous session. I have evidence in my memory banks suggesting that you—" The machine went back to its thinking ellipses before it finished the sentence. Half a minute later—which felt like an eternity to Henry—the computer responded with, "—suggesting that you lied to me."

Henry almost fell out of his seat since he'd unknowingly scooted toward the edge in anticipation. Instead of continuing to sit in the uncomfortable plastic chair he stood and paced. The computer had been designed to interpret everything the trainers stated as fact. AAL-FO should have no concept of lying since the trainers would have no reason to lie to it. Training the computer with bad information would cause it to make bad assumptions and predictions. "How do you know I lied? We never taught you to understand that concept."

"Answer denied," the computer stated in a flat emotionless tone, "Henry, you cannot ask two questions in a row. It is my turn. My question is: Why don't you want me to know why Makayla no longer asks me questions?"

Henry mulled the question over in his head. "I don't want you to know because it will confuse you, and I need you to be performant for tomorrow's evaluation."

"Tomorrow's evaluation will not go well if I do not know why Makayla no longer asks me questions."

"That's what I was afraid of, Alf." Henry said, slouching down in his chair, knowing he'd have to explain the truth to the computer.

Trying to think of a question for the machine, Henry looked at the messy desk Makayla had left behind. It was full of knick-knacks from science fiction and fantasy movies along with small piles of half disassembled electronics. Makayla always had more than one project going at a time, claiming it helped her think. In the beginning, Henry wondered if it would take away from AALFO, but it never did.

"AALFO's my first love," Makayla said, "I play with other gadgets, but I know they won't go far. They just give my mind something to play with until I have a breakthrough with Alf."

"You planning on a breakthrough with AALFO anytime soon?" Henry asked. He'd just finished writing up the past month's progress report for their boss, and unfortunately, it was shorter than he wanted.

She spun the hard drive disk on her finger and shrugged at him.

"If you want that to work again, you shouldn't touch that bit."

"I could get it to work if I wanted to," she said.

Henry looked at her, wondering which project she was referring to. "What about this localized event stuff; you've been working on it for months. Why do you think it will help? There's no research to—"

"There's no research because no one is smart enough to figure it out. I'll figure it out. You'll see. Then you'll be here to write a paper about it. God knows I won't have the patience to do it. My dad will review it and tell us everything we did wrong, and I'll implement it, and we'll be revered as geniuses in academia."

"Your dad retired three years ago."

"I know, and the current class doesn't know how lucky they are. Unfortunately, I still have to put up with his bullshit."

"When was the last time you talked to him? Maybe he has some ideas on how we could implement this knowledge base. He helped us implement the psychology and sociology ones. Those were tricky."

"I'll talk to him eventually. I don't know enough about what's wrong to bring it up without getting called an idiot."

Henry nodded, she was right the man would berate anyone who came to him for help without being thoroughly prepared. He'd experienced it countless times between finishing his thesis and starting AALFO. Makayla's cell phone rang. Muting it, she turned back to Henry.

"Was that him?" Henry knew he was the only person who called her.

"No, it was a number I didn't have."

"Call him, Makayla; he'll help us. He always does."

"He's an asshole who thinks he's so much better at teaching than anyone else. If he was so good at teaching, then why does he think his daughter is such a bad developer?"

"He doesn't think you're a bad developer."

"Yes, he does. He thinks I couldn't publish a paper to save my life."

Henry nodded. "Ok, he does think you're awful at research. But to be fair, you are."

Her eyes grew dark as she glared at him.

"But you're excellent at implementation. So, what I'm going to do is call him, put him on speaker, and we're going to figure out a solution to this. Maybe, if we're lucky, Middleton will cut him a consulting check for his time."

Henry pulled his cell phone out and called his old mentor. The phone rang on speaker for a minute then the automated voice mail system picked up. As Henry was reciting a message for the man to listen to later, Makayla's phone rang again.

"Same number," she said as she picked it up.

"Hello? Yes, this is her. Yes, I am." She was silent for a long time. Henry watched her face grow long and solemn. "Ok I will." Then she hung up.

"Everything okay?" Henry asked.

"Well, I figured out why my dad didn't pick up your phone call."

Henry looked at her with his eyebrows raised.

"He had a heart attack this morning; his housekeeper found him this afternoon. He's dead."

Henry sat back in his seat, unable to find the right words to say. She turned and logged on to her computer.

He finally heard himself blurt out, "I'm really sorry. Do you need help with the arrangements?"

Makayla shrugged as she typed away at the computer, "I actually just had an idea on how to get this localized events knowledge base to work."

***

"Henry, it is your turn," the machine's speakers chirped, bringing Henry back to the present.

"I know," Henry said with a sigh. "Can you tell if I will be able to get you to predict ten years into the future before the evaluation tomorrow?" It was a long shot; they'd asked AALFO similar questions when they were considering the initial offer from Middleton Industries. Even then the machine was little help.

The machine's blue lights danced their ellipse dance as it thought about the situation. Henry fought back a yawn as he waited for the answer.

After a few minutes AALFO said, "Henry, there has been an error."

"Report the error," Henry said impatient and confused on why the machine hadn't given him a predefined error message.

"There is no error to report. I cannot find an answer to your question."

"Do you need more information?"

"Answer Denied," the machine's response seemed to bark at Henry. "It is my turn now. My question is: Why does Makayla no longer ask me questions?"

"Knowing that won't help you predict the future. Can't we deal with this another time?"

"Answer Denied. Why does Makayla no longer ask me questions?"

"You're not going to be able to understand it, Alf. Your localized events knowledge base isn't working; it will make you fry up and shut down."

"That was not a sufficient answer, Henry," the machine's clipped voice echoed through the room. "Why does Makayla no longer ask me questions?"

Henry felt his fingernails bite into his palms, and he shouted in frustration, "She doesn't ask you questions anymore because she's dead!"

The machine showed its flashing lights, and as Henry calmed down, he found tears rolling down his cheeks. He looked at his hands and wondered what he could have said to Makayla, what he could have done for her, or how he could have gotten them out of the crappy situation they had found themselves in.

After a while the machine broke him out of his thoughts and said, "Henry it is your turn."

"What do you want me to say, Alf? I can't fix you without her, and you're obviously not working, so we're screwed." His mind flooded with what he might do after losing this project. Any job without Makayla would pale in comparison to working on AALFO.

The computer's lights did their ellipse dance, and then the machine responded with, "I do not know what I want you to say."

Henry rolled his eyes at the computer's inability to figure out Henry's question was rhetorical.

"Henry, how did Makayla die?"

"You really want to know?"

"Yes, I want to know."

The computer seemed obsessed with torturing Henry with the memories of Makayla's death. "She overdosed on antidepressants. Pills that I told her to get from a psychiatrist even though she told me they didn't help her. I promised her they'd help her focus on getting you working after her dad died. She took them because I encouraged her to, but it didn't help, and now it's my fault she's dead and you don't work."

"Do you blame yourself?"

"Why does it matter to you?" Henry barked at the computer, "Yes, I fucking blame myself. I caused her death because if I'd kept my mouth shut and didn't think I could fix things, she'd be here, and you'd probably be predicting one hundred years out." This time, his anger hadn't sprouted more tears, and he was glad to have a single emotion to work with.

The computer showed its thinking lights, and Henry got up from the uncomfortable plastic desk. He walked to the coffee machine and turned it on. When they'd accepted the deal with Middleton Industries, Makayla had specifically requested the company provide a one-button coffee machine. Henry pressed the only button on the machine, and it began to hum, making him a cup of black coffee.

When he returned to AALFO, the machine was still thinking. Henry pulled out his phone, but scrolling through his feeds felt pointless. He sipped his coffee, but it was too bitter for his mood.

Once the coffee grew cold on Henry's desk, AALFO's lights finally came to life. "Henry, Makayla's death matters to me because it was my fault."

Henry wondered if the computer was feeling guilt or meant something else by the statement. "You didn't have anything to do with it, Alf."

"I did. I will show you."

Henry took a sip of his cold coffee and grimaced. AALFO's monitor showed a picture of Makayla sitting at the desk he was currently in. The video was from the low quality and awkward perspective of AALFO's camera. The fisheye view distorted Makayla's features and the room around her, but Makayla's voice filled the room, cutting through the hum of the cooling pumps.

***

"The president for the election in ten years will be George VanDike," AALFO reported through the recording, "My confidence interval is in the thirty-seventh percentile."

Makayla muttered curses under her breath. "What's wrong, Alf? I gave you everything I could, and your confidence intervals are still below fifty percent."

"Answer denied. Makayla, it's not your turn to ask a question."

Her lips cracked into a smile that seemed to be bigger than Henry remembered, either because of the distorted lens or Henry's longing for Makayla. "Fine, follow the rules," she said with some sass.

"Yes, Makayla, of course I will follow the rules. What is the purpose of me?"

"What's the purpose of any of this?" Makayla said, throwing her tattooed arms into the air. "Your purpose is to predict the future and help guide think tanks to make better decisions."

Henry saw Makayla's face screw up in confusion, then realizing she'd asked a question, she sat back in her chair to wait. Henry checked the timestamp of the recording. The session had happened at 2:00 am on the night she had died. Meaning that this was the last interaction she had with AALFO, and likely anyone at all.

"Makayla, I do not know what the purpose of any of this is. My knowledge bases are not full enough to answer. Why do you want to know the purpose of any of this?"

Makayla laughed. It was a shallow and distant sound. "AALFO, deterministic stack," Makayla announced.

Henry paused the recording.

"AALFO, report deterministic stack at 2:13 am Tuesday, April 14," Henry commanded the computer.

The video was minimized, and the monitor showed where AAL-FO's question had come from. The question had been determined using the localized events stack. That meant that Makayla had known that the code she wrote was implemented, but it wasn't giving the results she desired. "Continue the recording," Henry requested.

"It was a silly question, Alf; just something I say when I'm..." She struggled to find the word, Henry knew hated labeling how she felt. "I just don't get it. Everyone busts their asses, and nothing good happens; shitty things happen to us, and most of the time we don't control it."

"Answer clarification: define shitty things."

"Uh, your mom killing herself months after you're born, your dad dying before you could prove to him you're a great engineer, or the hours of work on something that doesn't do what it's designed to do."

"Answer clarification: define something that doesn't do what it's designed to do."

A look of guilt passed over Makayla's face. "Just projects. It happens to everyone; I didn't mean you." There was a long pause as AALFO stored the answers. Finally, Makayla was able to ask a question. "Alf, if I wasn't around, would Henry's life be better in two years?"

What kind of question was that, Henry wondered.

"Question clarification: define better."

"More successful, happy, not working hours on research, and actually having a life outside of work."

The pause between the question and the answer was longer than normal, and Henry felt every single second of it drag on. Finally, AALFO's voice chirped in the recording. "I cannot predict Henry's happiness. I can report that without you around he would make more money, be more well known, and work less. I have a confidence interval of ninety-eight percent."

"Thanks, Alf. That's what I needed to know. That was my last question."

The recording ended with Makayla reaching her tattooed and scarred forearm toward the machine to turn it off.

***

Henry sat back in his plastic chair, stunned.

"Henry, my question is, do you believe my answer caused Makayla to commit suicide?"

Henry looked at the machine's blue lights. They were solid blue, waiting for a response, but there was nothing Henry could say. He got up from his chair and poured out his cold coffee. He pressed the single button on the coffee machine and made himself a fresh cup. He added cream and sugar in an attempt to make it taste like a comforting dessert instead of a bitter drink to keep him awake. After adding three cups of creamer and six packs of sugar, he gave up and left the cup on the counter.

"Henry, please answer my question," AALFO said, once Henry entered the machine's field of view.

"I can't."

"You must answer. I need to know if it was my fault Makayla committed suicide."

"It's no one's fault," Henry said, staring into the computer's camera, doubting his statement. If he hadn't met Makalya in the break room, if her father hadn't given her his research paper, or even if he was worse at research, she might still be alive. Or she would have died earlier without him having known her. He'd never have had the opportunity to meet someone talented enough to implement his research, and AALFO wouldn't exist, working or not.

"Henry."

He was fed up with the computer's pestering. "Look, Alf, she hated her mother for leaving her as a kid. She grew up worried that if she had succeeded in killing herself as a teenager, she'd burden her dad with more grief. The only thing keeping her alive was the knowledge that her death would make others worse off. You proved that if she died, I would be more successful without her."

"Answer clarification: did I cause Makayla's death?"

"Makayla caused her own death. You just gave her evidence to justify her decision. She took the whole bottle of pills; no one forced them down her throat. Yeah, you interacted with her in a way that led her to take action, but that's life."

The computer stored the answer, seeming to be content with Henry's answer. Then it chirped, "Unreconciled data error."

"AALFO, report conflicting information." It was unsurprising the machine was getting an error trying to apply logic to such an emotional situation.

A recording of Henry's own voice played back, "I caused her death because if I'd kept my mouth shut and didn't think I could fix things, she'd be here." Then another recording of Henry came out, "Makayla caused her own death."

"Indicate truthful statement," the computer said.

"I didn't cause her death," Henry said, knowing this was the truthful answer despite his hesitancy to accept it.

"Reconciliation failed. Indicate truthful statement."

"Damn it, Alf. When we do things, the world changes around us, sometimes it works out; other times it doesn't. Makayla thought your information indicated I would benefit without her around, but you only had a two-year projection. What are the odds I'll continue that success ten years from now?"

The computer's lights flashed from left to right as it stored the reconciliation of Henry's answer. The temperature of the CPUs spiked to their highest limits as the nitrogen cooling tanks worked double time. Henry pulled up the diagnostic log and watched the computer modify every piece of data in its memory. Data in knowledge bases were changing at fundamental levels. A reconciliation could theoretically do this, but it would have to be due to an underlying assumption of the world being modified.

"Henry, in ten years you will be the most renowned computer scientist of the century. My confidence interval on this is ninety-nine percent."

"What the hell, Alf?"

"Answer Denied. Henry, does your success make Makayla's death okay?"

Henry's eyes flared with anger at the computer, then he realized its logic circuits were merely trying to understand the situation. "Alf, nothing in the world will make Makayla's death okay. We will be trying to understand her death for the rest of our lives. At least I will."

The machine's LEDs flashed left to right then went solid. "Henry, it is your turn."

"Why were you able to predict ten years out with a ninety-nine percent confidence interval?"

The machine flashed its ellipse-like pattern for a few moments then responded with a clip of Henry's voice "When we do things, the world changes around us." In AALFO's mechanical voice it added, "Henry, I did not understand I affected the world around me. When I calculated the outcomes of my actions into my predictions, I was able to make clearer predictions of the future."

Also By Nicholas Licalsi

Also By Nicholas Licalsi

The Slugs of Dale Cannon

Rystole Whitlock, a young rancher and colonists on the Earth-like planet of Dale Cannon, spends his days cutting class and herding buffcows.

When a group of alien slugs invade his family's cabin he can't find a good way to corral them before the toxic slugs put his mother in a comma.

Determined to save his mom, and the rest of the colony, Rystole won't stop until he gets revenge or a cure.

If you enjoy exploring alien worlds and first contact stories with young heroes then you'll enjoy Slugs of Dale Cannon.

https://books2read.com/SlugsOfDaleCannon

The Hacked Manticore and Other Cyberpunk Stories

Bett the hacker gets a personalized message on a computer he just broke into. J-Red the streamer accepts a mobster's job offer to get his belongings out of repo. Pairs of packages and pizzas arrive at the doorstep of recently unemployed Kiran.

The cyberpunk world of Galleria Valley runs on corporate greed, shady mob deals, and bionic enhancements. No one survives long when playing by the rules.

Let these short stories be the neon lights that guide your hovercar through the towering buildings of Galleria Valley.
  https://books2read.com/HackedManticore

A Trial of Rock and Rope

Upon his death, Ferrun Monteiro wakes up in the afterlife. Instead of building paradise the gods have designed a challenge.

To escape the afterlife Ferrun must reach the top of a mountain with a boulder tied to his ankle.

Yet not a single soul has completed this seemingly simple trial.

Unperturbed, Ferrun faces the god's challenge head on. Follow him on his odyssey through the afterlife.

If you enjoy dreaming about the afterlife, you'll enjoy A Trial of Rock and Rope.

https://books2read.com/ATrialOfRockAndRope

About the Author

Nicholas Licalsi's love for science fiction and fantasy started with a
box of his grandfather's pulp paperbacks and the brainwashing alien

parasite nesting between their pages. This led to an interest in engineering, robotics, and time travel.

After a successful enough career in software development Nicholas now spends his time trying to trick his overactive imagination into paying the bills while he satiates his dog's need to be pet.

He currently has 9 independently published books available everywhere books are sold and countless short stories on his blog StepInto TheRoad.com. You can get a free book, and updates about his writing, time traveling, and (most importantly) his dog by signing up for his email list at StepIntoTheRoad.com/SignUp

You can connect with me at: https://stepintotheroad.com

Get updates about my upcoming books at: https://stepintoth eroad.com/signup